Stone Dead

Linda Menzies

© Linda Kathleen Menzies 2021

Cover illustrations by Jude Gordon

This is a work of fiction, and any resemblance to individuals, living or dead, is purely co-incidental. Real places have been used fictitiously.

Prologue

There was so little blood, it seemed impossible that she had died. The quarry tiled kitchen floor near her head had a smear of sticky, drying blood. Sam lay, looking as peaceful as if she was merely sleeping, and even in death, her beauty was undeniable and striking. That stunning face, which had broken so many hearts, was blanched and still; the wide blue eyes stared upwards, unseeing; her long, shapely legs splayed, slumped and inert. Her arms were crooked at odd angles, as if she'd tried to break her fall.

The women stood at the kitchen door, gazing in horror, a strange inertia freezing them into immobility as they took in the scene: the body, the signs of a scuffle, a broken plate and overturned chairs.

Maureen's nursing instinct overrode her revulsion at the scene, and she checked for signs of life, without disturbing the position of the body. "I'm afraid she's dead," she said, rising to her feet and rejoining the others at the doorway.

Jennifer broke the silence in a voice fractured with fear and bewilderment. "I'll call the police. We should leave everything as it is till they get here. "In silence, they moved out of the cottage and Jennifer secured the door with the master set of keys.

In the farmhouse courtyard, a bitter spring wind lashed the huddled group of women, who stood, stunned into a bleak silence. The stones of the old buildings groaned faintly in the wind. They'd known, felt the sinister stirrings, the malign feelings growing over the months until their ancient frames shuddered. Now it had happened, and she lay dead, her blood leaching into their fabric, their history.

The wind gathered pace and flung sharp sleet around the courtyard as night loomed down.

Chapter 1
The Farmhouse

The blank eyes of the farmhouse looked onto the dismal landscape, where daylight was fast failing over the churned winter fields. The odd shaft of the dying sun slid against the windows, making an odd, fiery blinking in the dead panes. A few gulls wheeled and called in mournful cacophony.

The old man moved a little in his chair, his weary eyes seeing not the fields he had worked for half a century, but a newly dug grave, topped by a simple granite headstone, engraved with gold lettering and with a space for another name below. For his name, when the time came.

"You'll be fine in the home, dad. There'll be company for you, you'll have all your meals made and someone on hand all the time to help you if you fall."

Isobel stood above her father, pulling each finger of her leather gloves into place with brisk intensity, and avoiding looking at him. Her voice was sharp, edgy, the tone of the teacher she was, used to dealing with awkward children.

"The estate agent will be coming over next week to value the properties and put the buildings up for sale." She paused, and added with false enthusiasm: "It's so lucky that the land isn't an issue. You'll be glad that George has bought the fields to add to his acreage!" The brittle cheerfulness in her voice resonated in the gloomy air.

Her father looked at her for the first time. "Well, George has always had his eye on my fields, ever since he took over from his dad at Whinneybraes. He's said a few times, 'John, will you not part with a few acres so I can expand?' "

'Well, good that the sale is settled," said Isobel, wrapping her thin, angular frame in a scarf and then a tweed coat. With that common, sudden rush of expansiveness which comes as a difficult encounter is about to end, and escape is in sight, she bent down and kissed her father's cheek. "The casserole is in the oven on a low heat, and that should do you today and tomorrow. I'll be back when the estate agent is here, and I'll help you sort out what you want to take with you to your new place... photos and suchlike."

John looked away, his face set and sad, and stared into the fire.

Once Isobel had driven away, John rose from his chair, leaning hard on his stick and wincing as the arthritis gripped his knees with a painful insistence. From the mantelpiece, he lifted the photograph taken on his wedding day. His beautiful Rose smiled out from the black and white print, one arm thrust through his and the other holding tightly to a bouquet of flowers. Sighing, he replaced the photograph and began the slow journey through to the kitchen to fill and boil the kettle.

"Well, I'm sure we'll be able to do something for you, Mr Scott. I'll draft up a proof of the sales brochure for you and we'll begin the marketing process as soon as possible." Ryan shifted his stance a little, glancing up at the old man from his clipboard. "This is a fine stone house, and I'm sure a buyer will be able to renovate the cottages and outbuildings."

The old man's sadness was palpable. "My father worked this land, and my grandfather before him," he said, his tone flat, with its acceptance of age and loss of power. "I've no laddie to leave it to, just the girls, and they're not interested in taking on a farm like this. I've never lived another place in my life!"

Ryan cleared his throat. Nobody had told him about this, the human side of his job. His career was all going to be brisk business, glossy brochures and nice commissions to fund his beach holidays and pay the mortgage on his own flat, a pristine glass and steel new build apartment in Dundee.

Instead, there was all this sad stuff, old ladies usually, not so many men, leaving their family homes to go into care or sheltered housing; or younger people losing their jobs and having to go into rented flats.

He'd intruded into children's bedrooms with stacked cartons, an Elsa doll from Frozen peeping over the top, peeling Goth posters in teenage bedrooms – what was that odour which instantly marked out the domain of a 15 year old boy? In tired rooms of houses where people were divorcing, he flipped his tape measure back and forth and jotted down particulars, while lives crumbled around him.

Chapter 2
The Women Meet

They sat on sagging sofas in the lounge of the cold, old fashioned hotel, not unlike others in the rural areas of Scotland which had resisted modernisation. The flock wallpaper cast a dispiriting gloom on the cool room, as did the heavily framed oil paintings lowering in the early winter evening. In a nearby room, a man in an ill-fitting lounge suit played bland music on a tinny keyboard. The smell of lentil soup drifted through from the adjacent dining room, where a waitress took orders from a few solitary diners.

The women, uneasy in the dispirited miasma, sipped tepid coffee and looked at one another with growing unease, their enthusiasm retreating. There had been desultory introductions followed by surreptitious glances as each of them assessed one another.

The double doors of the hotel lounge clanged open with a sudden crack, and all eyes turned to the woman who had just entered.

Jennifer's smile was the first thing you noticed. It seemed to flash around the dingy room, landing on each of the women in turn. Her blue shirt was peacock bright against her tanned skin and her suit jacket flashed open a little, showing the silken lining and bespoke tailor's label.

"Rather exotic for a country life," thought Elaine, "but then again, she's a London businesswoman…"

There was a faint stirring as Jennifer's energy invigorated the atmosphere. The women sat up straighter in their chairs, put down their coffee cups, and prepared to listen.

Jennifer took a seat and drew out a folder and pen from her briefcase.

"I'm Jennifer Armstrong and I'm so glad you are all here. Thank you for coming out on such a cold day!" She smiled again, flicking back a wisp of blonde hair and crossing her legs. "We should go round the table and introduce ourselves." One by one, Rose, Irene, Maureen, Frankie, Elaine and Jo gave their names, and a brief account of their situations.

"You've all signed up to a rather unusual living arrangement," Jennifer began. "As the estate agent will have explained, last year I purchased Barleyknowe farmhouse, the outbuildings, cottages and one field. Now that the renovation work is complete, I've sold five of the cottages to yourselves, and I've retained ownership of the farmhouse, barn and two of the cottages, plus the field."

She flicked over a page on the clipboard, looked up, and smiled again. "The barn will be used for storage of crops and equipment – yes, I hope we'll have some crops to store – and for communal gatherings. I'll rent out one of my two cottages on long lets, say one to two years maximum at a time, to a suitable woman who wants to paint, write, weave or simply get away from the world and be by herself, to rest and recharge her batteries."

A couple of the women listening to Jennifer exchanged looks.

"Don't worry, it'll be someone who will fit in to our lifestyle," Jennifer reassured them, catching the glances. "The second cottage will be kept for temporary guests, like your families and friends, and it will available rent-free, with just a nominal charge for heating costs."

"What about the field?" asked Jo. "Are we all expected to help with crops you mentioned?"

The slight concern in Jo's voice didn't go unnoticed by the younger woman.

"What I intend is that we can each have an area of the field to work, if we want it, to provide vegetables and soft fruits," explained Jennifer. "There will be communal projects too, perhaps a greenhouse and later on, some fruit trees, some beehives, hens and the like, but I intend a barter system to work here. "

"A barter system?" queried Elaine. "I'm a businesswoman, and would like to know just what that involves!"

Jennifer smiled at her. "That's a good question, and here's how I see it working. So, let's say, if one person wants to grow potatoes and carrots in their section, they can exchange these for some green beans or lettuce with their neighbour. Or someone less able for heavy work could cut a deal with the raspberry grower to make jam from soft fruits and share an exchange of jam for next door's beetroot."

Jennifer looked around them all again. "This way, the field will be put to good use and we can become more or less self-sufficient in vegetables and fruit. I haven't worked out the fine details, but that's roughly how I see it going."

Jennifer rested the clipboard on her knee and smiled at the women.

"We'll live both independently and communally, which sounds like a paradox, but I think it will work out well. You'll obviously come and go as you please, and live your own lives at Barleyknowe, but you'll also have the advantage of a community around you for company if you want it, and sharing of common tasks like using the field, as I've outlined. We'll need to take turns weeding and sweeping the common courtyard, but apart from that, there's nothing too onerous or intrusive. I'll run a communal diary to let you all book out the guest cottage and so on."

Jennifer paused. "No doubt some of you are wondering how this will work out, and I expect your lawyers have pored over the more unusual clauses in the title deeds. Basically, you are free to sell up at any time, provided that your purchaser is a woman."

She held up her hand. "Yes, this is unusual I know, but it's all been checked out under discrimination legislation and we are able in law to put in this clause."

She consulted her folder. "There are a small number of practicalities and details still to be finalised. For example, my house will be known as Barleyknowe Farmhouse and the cottages are numbered one to seven Barleyknowe Farm Cottages, but it's perfectly fine if you also want to give your new home a name as well."

She looked at the attentive women. "For instance, Jo and Maureen will be living in the pair of cottages made from the old dairy, so you can take that as a steer for names, if you like.
"The two guest cottages have been formed from what was the stable block, so I need to think of suitable names for numbers six and seven Barleyknowe Farm Cottages.
" I'll be putting together a welcome pack for all of us, and for our short-term guests, with some information about bin collections, local services like dentists and doctors and such like, as I understand none of us are local to this area. I'm looking forward to us all being neighbours, and hopefully, friends in time. Now, please help yourselves to more coffee, and I'll catch up with you all at Barleyknowe. I have to drive back to Edinburgh to catch a late flight back to London, so this has to be a short meeting, but we'll all be in touch by email, and please ask any questions, or have your lawyers contact mine."

With another flashing smile which didn't quite meet her eyes, Maureen noticed, Jennifer gathered up her briefcase and handbag, and walked smartly out through the doors, a leaving a trace of expensive perfume in her wake.

There was a brief silence before the women began to speak in a low murmur, their cups chinking in the dismal room.

"Where did she get the cash to buy the place and do it all up in the first place?" Irene voiced the question they all had in mind.

Maureen put down her cup and saucer and looked across at Irene.

"I believe she works in the financial sector in the city of London, but is planning to relocate to Barleyknowe and do some consultancy work from home. Semi-retirement, I guess, which is what these high fliers do: make a wad of cash then live the life they really want!" She smiled ruefully. "Nice if you can pull it off!"

"I heard that she inherited a property in London and used the proceeds to buy the farm," ventured Elaine.

"Maybe both stories are true," ventured Jo. "Does it really matter? We'll find out what we need to, and what she wants us to know, when we get to know each other. I for one am glad she came up with this plan, and I'm looking forward to moving in and starting this new life!"

Her comments altered the atmosphere, and all the women visibly relaxed.

"It's going to be fun!" said Frankie, who till now had sat quietly, listening to the ebb and flow of conversation. The youngest of the group by many years, she was an exotic bird in a flock of sparrows with her pink silk shirt, cutaway jeans and Rocket Dog rainbow trainers. Her long dangly earrings, make-up and wild, curly hair competed the picture of a young, vibrant person.

"Fun!" Maureen smiled inwardly at the naïve choice of words. "A child, cultivating a Bambi demeanour and fey, arty-farty appearance to hide a certain city street-wise awareness. She probably has mummy or daddy issues and is shockingly untidy, and useless with money," she thought wryly. "I wonder how long she'll last up here in rural Angus!" Then, she rebuked herself for her cynicism. "Stop it, Maureen," the kinder part of her brain chided. "She's probably a lovely young woman, you don't know her history, so just hold back on the criticisms till you've actually got something to complain about!"

She replaced her cup and saucer on the shabby coffee table and smiled across at Frankie. "Well, it's certainly going to be different!" she said. "It'll be a new way to live, for me, anyway. I have a few pangs about leaving Edinburgh, but…"

Frankie cut in: "Oh, you're in Edinburgh! Me too, I'm in a flat in Meadowbank at the moment, but so looking forward to a lovely peaceful life up here…peaceful but fun!"

Maureen smiled again, and said no more. Time would tell if Frankie was going to be a good neighbour and an energising asset to the community, or a gigantic, needy, pain in the butt.

Ice broken, the women chatted freely, talking of their dates to move in, their reasons for choosing this life style and a little of their present circumstances. After an hour or so, they began taking their leave, with promises to keep in touch before moving into their new homes. There was a quick exchange of email addresses and phone numbers, and Frankie suggested that they form a private Facebook group so they could share information as they drew nearer to moving-in day.

There were a few glances of veiled surprise at this suggestion.

Frankie chuckled. "Yes, I told you that I was an artist and amateur musician, and that's true, but my day job is computer programming. I did an IT qualification when it was obvious I couldn't live by painting alone, and that work is what keeps the wolf from the door and hopefully will do so at Barleyknowe too! I'll set up a private Facebook group for us if you like, it won't take me long."

Maureen's inner voice spoke up again. "Told you before, don't judge by appearances, don't second guess. You put this young woman in a pigeonhole and actually, she doesn't fit the box you chose for her, just like many people, there are different sides to her. Stop being so judgmental!"

Oblivious to this inner dialogue, Frankie smiled at Maureen again.

"Are you going back to Edinburgh tonight?' she asked.

"No, I've booked into a hotel in Forfar for the night. I'll drive back down tomorrow."

"I've got a B&B in Arbroath," said Frankie. "It was just a bit far to drive home tonight. I'm looking forward to an Arbroath smokie for breakfast tomorrow, and maybe an Aberdeen buttery to go with it: I need to get to know all the local delicacies!"

Maureen smiled back at the younger woman.

"Thank heavens she isn't in the same hotel as me," said the grumpy part of her brain. "We'd be up all night while she told me her life story, I'll bet!'

***

Rose and Irene rose simultaneously from the sofa, with the synchronicity of years of habit and connection and took their leave of the others. Outside in the frosty, bleak car park, lit only by fuzzy orange lamps, they climbed quickly into their Fiesta and Irene negotiated the car out into the country road. The hedgerows loomed high and dark and the cat's eyes provided a glittering pathway along the snow-dusted roadway.

Rose waited until they reached the well-lit motorway and were safely on the road home to Perth before breaking the silence.

"What did you make of all that, then?" she queried.

Irene indicated to overtake a slow-moving lorry before replying.

"Not sure yet. Jo seems a friendly sort, and it's always nice to be in the company of another lesbian. My Gaydar began pinging the minute she walked in! Not sure about the boss lady, Jennifer, what did you make of her?"

Rose stared out of the window at the dark, empty fields.

"She's what she is, Irene: a successful, wealthy woman who sees this community living as a lucrative experiment which will suit her needs, whatever they are. No doubt we'll find out more as time goes by. I'm wondering if she's of a Sapphic bent too?"

Irene exclaimed impatiently. "For god's sake! Stop using this ironic, formal language, Rose! It really grates on my nerves sometimes. Do you think you're on a Radio 4 culture programme? Just ask me if I think she's a dyke too!"

Both women fell silent, and in the edgy closeness of the car, Rose turned again to look out of the window, her flushed face half-hidden as she stared out at the dark fields, which were studded with occasional lights from farm cottages. Flurries of snow showed in the car's headlights, and they both glanced at a gritting lorry rumbling along the north-bound carriageway. The car's engine droned faintly as they travelled through the night.

Say nothing, show no reaction, Rose reminded herself silently. Irene's temper could flare at the slightest provocation, or at none at all. Her unpredictability had been one of her charms at first, she was exciting, fun and spontaneous…

"When did I start to fear her?" Rose wondered, watching the darkling landscape speed past. "Was it when she broke my favourite ornament, the china cat the grandchildren gave me, throwing it down on the tiled hall floor where it shattered into all those tiny shards, completely beyond fixing, just because I'd forgotten to stop by the shop for milk? Or was it that awful night when I came in later than expected from a night out with friends, and she'd been brooding and watching the clock, and turned on me in a rage the moment I walked in the door? As if I'd ever dream of cheating on her!"

Her reverie was broken as Irene said quietly: "I'm sorry, Rose. I'm a little tense about all of this and wonder if we're doing the right thing."

Rose hesitated before replying, glancing carefully at her partner's profile. "Well, you were really keen on the idea, Irene. It was me who had reservations at first about leaving our bungalow, our lovely garden and our friends and neighbours…" she tailed off.

Irene slowed the car, took the turn off to Perth and replied: "Yes, yes, of course I know really that we're doing the right thing. It's an ideal set-up for us. We'll have a manageable home, spanking new inside but with good stone walls and a bit of history to the place, as well as the company of a community with at least one other lesbian nearby. The bungalow is really too big for us now and the garden is becoming so hard for us to keep these days. Besides, Barleyknowe has guest cottages if ever we needed the space…"

This time, it was Irene who stopped the conversation, aware that dangerous waters were approaching, with this mention of visitors.

Katherine, James, Iona and Finlay: forbidden names, and visitors a taboo subject, too painful to discuss.

Rose bit her lip, but stayed silent. That particular can of worms was staying firmly closed tonight. Things were strained enough without that issue being aired, although maybe living at this new place would give them a chance to come to some sort of peace and understanding, a fresh start and a way to sort out old problems…

The two women sat in silence, the engine's quiet thrum the only noise, as they approached their street, then pulled into their driveway. Quietly, they opened the car doors and let themselves into the house which had been their home together since they left Glasgow all those years ago, to start a new life together in Perth.

Leaving Katherine behind.

***

Back at the hotel, Jo and Elaine shared a final cup of coffee in the empty lounge before setting off for their homes.

"How's the road to Aberdeen tonight?" Elaine enquired of Jo as they drained their cups.

"I'll just check," Jo replied, opening her phone and clicking on the travel app. "The motorway is clear, though it's still snowing," she said a moment or two later. "I'll get going shortly, and will be sticking to the main roads. You should be ok getting back to Dundee, Elaine, the A90 isn't showing any major issues."

"Ok, I'll not linger either," Elaine replied, collecting her handbag and coat.

The two women walked out to the car park together and shook hands.

"See you in a couple of months at Barleyknowe," said Jo. "I'm looking forward to this new life. It'll be different, anyway!"

"Yes, it certainly will," said Elaine, unlocking her car door.

With a final wave, the women headed in a convoy of two out into the swirling, snowy night air.

***

In the main lounge, a man closed the lid of the piano and tucked his sheet music into the piano stool's cavity before loosening his tie and moving wearily towards the bar, where the solitary barman was polishing glasses.

"Usual, Archie?" he asked the musician.

"Aye, make it a double, ta. Need something to help me walk home through that snow."

George chuckled. "You live five minutes' walk away, Archie! Off Forfar High Street, you're not on an expedition to the Antarctic!"

"Aye, but I've Jean to face as well as the snow. She found out about Katrina who was singing here last month and now I'm in the doghouse, yet again."

"Well, you should've been more discreet, Archie. You're a fool to yourself, sometimes," George smiled, pouring out a measure of whisky.

"Aye, an old fool too," agreed Archie, sighing deeply. There had been a time when he could have any woman he chose, and often did have any woman he wanted, but he'd usually tried to be discreet and careful, and kept these dalliances away from his home. Was he getting too old for this malarkey? he wondered, sipping his drink. Maybe he should just settle for what he had: a wife he was fond of, though hadn't loved for many years now. "She's familiar, but so's an old pair of slippers!" he thought, then quickly reproached himself for that thought. Then there were their two sons and three grandkids, who he loved with all his heart. His mojo was beginning to wane, no doubt about that. Was the thrill of the chase worth the hassle, the reproaches and the threat of losing all he had? No, probably not, he reflected, draining his glass and bidding the barman goodnight.

As he trudged along Forfar High Street through the falling snow, he mused on the twists and turns his life had taken. "If I hadn't got Jean pregnant I'd have been off to music college and who knows how my life would have turned out?"

The teenagers had what was known in those days as a shotgun wedding, Jean's parents insisting that they marry before the baby was born. Archie, who was at an FE college doing entrance qualifications with a view to study music at university, had abandoned his course and found full-time work with an insurance company in Dundee.

"Safe, but very dull," he remembered with some bitterness. "That job paid the bills, but it shrivelled my soul. All those tedious figures and spreadsheets! The best thing that ever happened to me there was the firm being taken over and me being offered early retirement." He had dutifully started work, earning to support his young wife and baby, but his music was, from then onwards, confined to playing piano or guitar in pubs and clubs to make some extra cash.

"Well, my lad, you should have kept it in your pants or used a condom!" he told himself ruefully, turning off the main road down into a smaller street which led to his house. "But then you'd not have had your laddies."

Putting the key in his door and entering quietly, so as not to disturb Jean, he hung up his snow-dusted coat and removed his boots, putting them carefully on the waiting newspaper to dry out. Winter in Angus, as in many communities in the north east of Scotland, brought out the newspaper ritual in every house in the county: the local daily paper had a second-day function mopping up wet shoes and boots.

But, hang on, Archie thought, climbing the stairs to his bedroom across the landing from the one he shared in the past with the now slumbering Jean, there had been a fine looking woman there tonight in that group having some sort of business meeting about moving into new housing development outside the town somewhere. Elaine, someone had called her, and he noticed her ringless left hand when he passed through the lounge on his way to the Gents.

Chapter 3
Settling In

February 2010

The sky menaced, lowering over the Angus fields. Now and then, a new, dark finger of cloud joined the heavy canopy. The rich soil was dusted with the snow of late February, which lay, intransigent, over the earthy furrows of the ploughed fields.

Snow stayed and settled in that part of the world, not with quite the ferocity and harshness seen further up into rural Aberdeenshire and the Grampians, but still asserting its dominance over daily life.

The people who lived there noted the seasons keenly and had respect for the weather, which could disrupt daily lives in hours. Flash floods hauled earth from the fields into the narrow country roads, creating treacherous mud, rivuleting, brackish torrents and huge, pooling swathes of water. In winter, ice landed early and stayed till spring, freezing stagnant water, ponds and the fringes of grey- green lochs and streams, breaking up the road surfaces and cracking open ice-glazed potholes.

Snow drove down from the Angus Glens, settling in the towns and villages, the farms and hamlets, the school playgrounds and side streets, landing on gardens and roof tops, dusting the fur of cats hurrying indoors, piling by centimetres on dustbin lids, sheds and street benches, turning grass white and clean and burying shrubs in pristine blankets.

A woman in Kirriemuir searched the darkening sky as she rose from the table, setting down her teacup, opened the kitchen door and hurried outside to begin unpegging sheets from her washing line. "That's it going to start again, and a bad one from the looks o' those clouds," said her neighbour, who was bringing in logs from a covered store next to her back door. "You ok for milk and suchlike?" she asked, a rhetorical question only designed to show friendly concern.

Everyone in the Angus towns and hamlets stocked up in readiness for wintertime. It was foolhardy not to be prepared for the weeks when getting around was difficult, when shops ran low on supplies and children revelled in extra time at home when the schools were closed and neighbours kept a watchful eye on elderly neighbours.

***

Fifteen miles away, Jennifer turned her windscreen wipers to fast and cursed under her breath. What had possessed her to move into Barleyknowe in winter? Another month or so wouldn't have made any difference: she still had three months to go on the lease of her flat in London and could easily have afforded to stay in a hotel for a few weeks if need be, but she wanted to move in before the other women started to arrive.

At last, through the swirling snowflakes, she spotted the hand-carved wooden sign with Barleyknowe written in deep, moss-encrusted letters, atop a field fence post, and made the left turn along the uneven, rutted farm track. The outlook was bleak, a lowering, menacing, cloud-packed sky shedding relentless flakes down onto the fields, outbuildings and the sheep huddled in distant fields.

Jennifer drew the car to a halt in the courtyard outside the farmhouse, and made a dash to the stout oak front door. Fumbling in her handbag for the key, she let herself into the silent hallway, scooping up mail and switching on the lights as she went through into the kitchen.

With swift competence, Jennifer turned up the central heating, which the builder had left on at low in the empty house. "Dinnae tak' any chances, lass," he told Jennifer over the phone. "The winter weather comes hard and sudden here, and lasts a good while. You'll no' want caught out wi' burst pipes before you've even moved in." Amused at his informality with a client who'd spent a fast amount of money with his firm, Jennifer agreed he should set the heating and hot water timer to come on for a few hours each day in the farmhouse and the other cottages.

Shaking the final drops of melting snow from her hair and hanging up her waxed jacket in the utility room, Jennifer then unpacked, filling the freezer, fridge and cupboards with provisions, finally dumping her suitcase in the bedroom along with a sleeping bag and an air bed to do her overnight.

"Camping indoors, what a novelty!" she mused. Last time she'd done that was when she'd fled from Vanessa's house, all those years ago. The last time she'd run away anywhere, away from anyone, and that was never going to happen again, she'd vowed. She'd lain shivering on her friend Susie's floor that night, curled into the sleeping bag she'd grabbed, turning over the horror of the final, hideous row with the woman who'd been her lover and partner for so long.

The searing, blistering crudeness and cruelty of Vanessa's drunken rant would stay with her for a long time. The things she'd said couldn't be undone, or unheard.

"You fucking fat cow! Who do you think you are, better than me, you snooty bitch! Holier than thou, pretending to be so perfect and there's you with a bastard son out there somewhere… I hate you!"

Vanessa's words had burned Jennifer, because there was some truth in the torrent of hateful words. She was aloof, and didn't suffer fools gladly. She could be bossy, she knew that, but where does assertiveness and confidence end and bossiness begin? Whatever you called it, it had helped her progress in her career, but the confidence seemed to fly out of the window when trying to deal with her partner.

The fat jibe had hit home hard, though, and there was no use trying to excuse her comfort eating by telling herself she was stressed out of her mind living with Vanessa. There was only one person responsible for what she ate, and that was herself, Jennifer. Once she had broken free of the toxic lifestyle with a controlling partner, turning to a healthy diet and making regular trips to the gym soon sorted out the excess pounds.

Now, she could look at herself in the mirror with satisfaction, knowing she was who and what she wanted to be.

Vanessa's cruel words about the baby had hit home though, and struck her very hard. Not a single day passed that she didn't think about the infant she'd given up for adoption, the painful parting from her son, that last kiss on his tiny forehead before the social worker took him away, and the tears she'd shed in her bedroom, for days and months afterwards. One of her major regrets was ever telling Vanessa that painful secret, but you should be able to tell the person you love everything, and know you won't be judged, only supported. Instead, the admission had been used against her, Jennifer recalled, unpacking toiletries in the bathroom.

"Forget it. That was a long time ago, she can't hurt you now." The inner voice of reason intervened, and Jennifer pulled herself into the present, and into her new life and new home, which stood solid against the snowy Angus night.

Tomorrow, her furniture and other possessions would arrive; she'd organise the Wi-Fi, phone connections and the hundred and one other things involved in moving home.

"Snagging list, first thing," she muttered to herself, buttering bread to have with the tin of soup heating on the Aga. "Stop thinking out loud, Jen!" she ruefully reproached herself, stopping to fish out a small portable radio from her suitcase. Soon, the anodyne and familiar sounds of The Archers theme tune echoed, then filled in the silence.

An hour later, after a shower taken to warm her through and also to check that the hot water supply was functioning, Jennifer set her phone alarm for 6am, blew up her air bed and snuggled into her sleeping bag. Tomorrow was a new day, and the start of her new life in Barleyknowe.

As she slept, cosy in the sleeping bag, the snow fell soft and silent outside, the wind dropped to a whisper, and above, light came faintly from the black velvet sky which was studded with stars. A hazy moon shone through moving clouds, and in nearby fields, an owl hooted, its voice eerie in the folds of night.

At Barleyknowe, the stones of each old cottage breathed out their secret histories to the neighbouring house, remembering the people who had lived and died there, suffered and laughed, given birth, fought and forgiven their neighbours' shortcomings, putting their differences aside to deal with harsh weather, ailing livestock and failing harvests. The odd, lingering sound leached faintly from the walls as memories were stirred in the snowy desolation, but the noises were so faint, so fleeting, that Jennifer's sleep was undisturbed. The houses, although modernised and repainted, were stubbornly intact, bearing the imprint and story of the whistling, cloth capped Victorian stone mason who created them with hammer, chisel and mortar mix. The cottages had seen a range of human frailties and kindnesses since then, but this was a new stage in their lives and something quite unexpected was about to unfold.

They settled down to wait.

Several days later, after a return visit from a plumber to fix a leaking toilet and a dripping tap, and from a joiner to adjust a couple of door handles and the back door lock, Jennifer had finished unpacking all her possessions and loaded up the car with cardboard boxes to take to the recycling plant, and do a few errands in Forfar.

Driving carefully along the farm road through Christmas cake icing snow, she made a mental note to look into having the private road cleared by a local farmer with a plough on his tractor. They all needed to be able to get to the main road in safety, whatever the weather. And they'd be starting to arrive from tomorrow.

Chapter 4
Rose McKay and Irene Fraser

"Do you really think that we're doing the right thing?" Rose put down the pile of photo frames she was holding, pushed back a tendril of grey, wispy hair and looked anxiously at Irene, who stood up straight from the box of china she was wrapping in newspaper."Of course we are, Rose! It makes sense to downsize and move to this community while we still have our health. We've discussed this endlessly, this is no time to have a wobble! Besides, this place is well and truly sold, we move out next week there's no going back now!" Irene's voice had the tinge of impatience Rose dreaded to hear.

"Och, I'm just being silly, I know," Rose replied, with a faint laugh, ignoring the start of the grinding, tightening feeling in her guts. At all costs, she must keep the peace which was so important to her well-being. She must humour Irene, and also keep a grip on her own temper which could, on rare occasions, flare unexpectedly high and bright when she was provoked, usually by Irene.

An interesting life was fine, but a volatile and troubled existence was abhorrent. After all that had happened, everything that they'd endured, they deserved a harmonious life together. "The Connor family will love living here and I know we're going to have a great time at Barleyknowe. There's going to be a lot less housework for one thing!"

The argument deflected, they turned back to their tasks in silence.

Chapter 5
Elaine Turner

1990

She found his wedding ring lying on the floor in the morning, next to the chair, and where his ashtray overflowed onto the carpet.

The worn gold band glinted reproachfully from where it lay, the lettering on the inside of the rim still retaining its brightness, showing their names, Michael and Elaine, and the date of their wedding some fifteen years earlier.
Her inner voice started up, that voice she'd tried to ignore for so long now.
"You don't take off your wedding ring without good reason. However you cut it, it's a significant and symbolic move, especially just after your wedding anniversary, with all the cards still on the mantelpiece!

Yet again, he's ignored the date, there's been no card, no gift, not even a 'happy anniversary' greeting! When are you going to wise up, lady! He doesn't love you, he feels trapped, he wants away but is only staying because he's no place else to go, you pay the bills and keep him…and maybe it's for Billy."

Sighing, and trying to shut off the depressing dialogue in her head, she went into the kitchen, set the kettle on to boil and then climbed back upstairs to waken Billy for school.

Sipping tea, she picked up the ring and put it on the coffee table next to the socks he'd taken off the night before and discarded for her to take to the laundry bin. Well, he could put his own dirty clothes in the bin. She wasn't a servant.

As she reversed out of the driveway, she sensed Billy's tense form next to her in the passenger seat and caught the sadness emanating from him, along with the overdose of deodorant, a common feature of teenage boys as they go from body-swerving baths to constantly showering and changing their clothes.

Elaine glanced back at the house and saw their bedroom blinds still drawn down. The familiar, daily knot in her stomach began to form, as she slipped the clutch and drove off to drop Billy at school, before going onto her own job in the salon.

The blinds would stay closed all day, as they usually did. The blank fabric, covering the eyes of the window, stayed still and silent in their reproach.

She glanced across at her son, sitting in the passenger seat, his head bowed and hands clenched together so tightly that his knuckles looked bone-white. The nape of his neck showed above his shirt collar, pink and achingly vulnerable.

It was time to form a plan, to take action, to stop living this dreadful, miserable life, for her sanity, and for Billy's sake.

***

2009

"Yes, I'm fine, keeping well. A bit of news though, I'm thinking of moving out to the countryside, to Angus, what do you think?" Elaine looked out of her salon window into the familiar Dundee street, which was busy with Friday morning shoppers, as she spoke on the 'phone.

"Are you sure that's what you want, mum?" Billy asked, swivelling back round to his desk again, and doodling with a pen on his blotter. "I thought you loved that flat of yours up the Perth Road." Subconsciously, he noticed that one of his office's window blinds was still down. Phone still to his ear, he pulled the chord to draw the blind open. An odd quirk, he knew, and one which made his wife Fiona laugh.

"I don't know why we have to open all the curtains and blinds first thing, Billy, even in the dead of winter! One of these days the window cleaner is going to catch me getting dressed!" Fiona said.

He'd laughed it off, saying he just liked the house to be alive first thing and not slumbering while they were all awake. His wife didn't need to know everything from his childhood. All that was in a locked box in his head, which he opened now and then in his darker moments, sifting through the memories, as if he was taking the band off a pile of old letters. The top one on the ghastly pile was coming home that day and finding his dad in bed with the woman from four doors along, and having to keep it all secret from his mum. "I'll batter you to kingdom come and back again if you say even just one word to your mother," his dad had roared at the scared boy. "And don't you go blabbing about anything else that's my business either! Nothing to do with you who comes into this house, or what I do, just you keep your bloody head down and your fucking wee gob tight shut!"

At the time, he'd never told anyone about just how terrible and miserable his father had made life at home, with his bullying, arrogant ways, his laziness and complete contempt for his wife and child.

"Maybe just as well I had a breakdown at University," he'd mused one day. "At least that kicked in the counselling and helped me process some of the stuff in my head!'

Turning away from the past to the present and future, Billy listened to his mother more intently.

"I'd like a small bit of garden, some outside space and a peaceful change of scene to come home to at night," she was saying. "I can manage the stairs to the flat fine just now, but I'm looking ahead to when I won't be so nimble.

"There's going to be a community at Barleyknowe and I like the sound of that. I'll have privacy in my own home and garden, but there'll be the company of neighbours and some things we'll work at together. I'll be coming into Dundee every day anyway, so it won't feel like being cut off from everyone."

"Well, if you think it's the right move for you, mum. Goodness knows you've worked hard enough over the years, buying your flat and building up your businesses…" Billy tailed off, then changed the subject.

"How's the new salon working out, by the way? Is the manager up to it?"

"Yes, she's very competent," his mother replied. "Young, of course, and full of new ideas, but that'll suit the clientele in the new shop. We've installed a nail bar and the décor's been modernised: it's all retro pastel shades and mirrors with stage dressing room-type lights round them, you get the picture, I'm sure! My more traditional clients will still come to me here in Dundee, or go to the other salon in Broughty Ferry, where we'll still offer perms and shampoo and sets."

Billy laughed. "Well, you know what your various ladies like! Let me know how you get on with the cottage, mum, and send me the weblink to the development." Billy's tone became brisker as his PA laid a pile of folders on his desk. "I need to go now, but let's fix a date for you to visit us soon. Charlie and Grace are always asking when Gran Scotland is going to come and see them again. I'll do the usual and pick you up at Manchester airport, unless you're thinking of taking the train this time?"

The call ended and Elaine turned again to the glossy pages of the estate agent's brochure.

Chapter 6
Jo Newton

Jo stared at the trees in the park across the road from her house, watching the branches move slightly in the wind.

A year. It had been a full twelve months since Wendy died. The seasons had come and gone in a blur of grief, of arrangements, sending back junk mail, taking clothes to the charity shop, answering condolence letters, and trying to make sense of it all, when there was really no sense to be made. The sadness was always with her, a solid stone in her gut, which she carried around while she attended to mundanities, met up with friends and passed the time of day with neighbours.

In those last days, at the hospice, Wendy urged her to move on. "There's plenty of life still for you, sweetheart," she said, her voice reedy and faint. "Don't use your time and your energies grieving for me. We've had a great life together, none better, and now you need to think ahead, about your life after me."

Jo's throat constricted at the memory. Together since their twenties, she and Wendy had battled for women's rights, stayed briefly in a commune, pitched camp at Greenham Common, and lived their lives in increasing openness as society shifted to a general acceptance of gay people.

Now it was time to pack up and leave what had been their home together for so many years, to reduce and declutter, and take only the most cherished and necessary items to her new home at Barleyknowe.

Jo sighed, and looked around the sitting room, where they'd sat cosily before the log fire on peaceful evenings, playing Scrabble, reading or knitting, as the various dogs and cats they had over the years had slumbered, soporific.

"Well, this lot isn't going to pack itself," Jo said out loud. That was the problem of living with someone all your adult life, you were so used to having someone to listen and respond, that it was a hard habit to break.

She pulled over the first of the waiting, empty cartons and began carefully filling it with books destined for the charity shop. As she systematically cleared the book shelves, she arrived at Wendy's collection of poetry books, neatly arranged in alphabetical order and including the two pamphlets Wendy had published of her own work, many years earlier. Jo opened one of pamphlets and flicked through the pages. In truth, Jo wasn't a poetry enthusiast, and although encouraging of Wendy's efforts, she had honestly never read her partner's work with any concentration. Skim reading, it had been, she admitted to herself.

Sitting on the floor, Jo began to read the poems, carefully and thoroughly.

***

An hour later, with a sick anguish rising in her, Jo rose to her feet and, tears blinding her, walked slowly over to the sideboard and pulled out the bottle of whisky they'd kept to make hot toddies when colds struck.

The bottle was two-thirds empty, most recently used to give Wendy a nightly tot as the cancer took over and before she moved to the hospice for her final days.

Her hand shaking, Jo poured a large tumbler-full, a bit of her brain thinking it was only ten in the morning.

Wendy had known all along, and hadn't said anything. Not a word had she uttered – there had been no gesture of reproach or anger, and there was no change in her behaviour, she was just the sweet and lovely person she'd always been.

Even at the very end, in her last moments, holding Jo's hand, she was thinking of her partner and her well-being, not of herself and what she must have endured and suffered.

But how had she found out?

Jo refilled the tumbler. The whisky was already taking effect, her tears flowed freely now. That bitch Karen had promised revenge at the time, and she must have found a way to get to Wendy, despite Jo's anguished pleadings, cajolings and even threats. Or was it Karen's spiteful act of revenge?

Could there be another explanation? Thinking about it now, all their poetry loving friends must have twigged too, when they read Wendy's collections. This could explain why some of that circle of friends were a little distant, even offhand with Jo after Wendy's pamphlet publication launches. At the time, she'd put this down to intellectual snobbery and elitism. Jo was a computer programmer, not interested in the arts and some of Wendy's pals were a little dismissive of her skills set, she knew. But prior to the first pamphlet launch, they'd always been friendly, at least. Now, it all seemed to make sense.

Nobody who hadn't experienced, at first hand, betrayal, humiliation, anguish and fear of loss could possibly write the words Jo had just read.

How could she have been so blind, so insensitive and stupid not to see what she now saw, written in black and white, Wendy's utter depths of pain and despair?

Sitting nursing the tumbler, and wishing she hadn't stopped smoking all those years ago, things began to click into place. Wendy's excessive grief over the death of their beloved dog Shula, which happened not long after Jo had ended the affair with Karen, now made sense. They had both loved the old spaniel, bought as a puppy when they bought their first home with a garden together, but Wendy's overwhelming, prolonged and vocal grief seemed extreme.

"Sweetheart, she was a very old dog and had a great life with us," Jo had comforted Wendy. "We both knew how sick she was towards the end. We did the right thing to have her put to sleep: the vet told us it was the only humane thing to do for her. We can have another dog one day, once we've got over the loss of Shula."

"I know, I know," Wendy had cried, her reddened, tear-drenched face looking at Jo. "It's just that I loved her so, so much and now she's been taken away from me, and there's this terrible, aching loss inside me."

Even at the time, Jo had wondered at the choice of words Wendy used, as well as this disproportionate cascade of grief. Now, it made perfect sense. It was Jo who'd been taken away from Wendy, and Shula was the embodiment of the loss of their contented lives together.

Still slumped on the floor, Jo remembered that insane chapter in their happy life together. Guilt flared in her anew. Why had she done it? Why had she started the affair with Karen?

Funnily enough, the first, noticeable altered behaviour was in her eating habits.

Jo felt the consequences one day when putting on her favourite blue checked shirt. There was a tiny straining and rucking across the stomach. Then, the zip caught on her jeans and she had to breathe in hard to tug it closed.

Weight gain seemed the least likely problem to have during an affair. You'd have thought all the extra sex, not to mention all the rushing around involved, would have burned off some of the calories. But no.

Talking out loud to the empty room, the whisky making her garrulous, Jo remembered.
"Heavens, I ate the big steak and kidney pies, bowls of pasta and creamy puddings which Wendy made me. Then I had to slip out on a pretext and drive to Karen's house, where she'd made me a Caesar salad, cheese cake, and those fruit platters she concocted!"
"You don't need to make me a meal, Karen," I'd protested every time. "I've eaten already, I had a big lunch!" Pointless. She wanted to keep me and did it through food and sex. And I loved it. What better accompaniment to lovemaking than champagne and strawberries dipped in chocolate?

"Hell mend you, Jo, why are you doing this?" My pal Doreen didn't mince her words when I confided in her. "Cheating on that lovely woman Wendy! This will end in tears." I couldn't help myself though.

Wendy and I had been together for fifteen years. We had the house, our succession of pets and a time share in Portugal. So maybe things had got a bit stale, a bit flat and predictable in the bedroom? We were an old married couple. Wendy was brilliant, supporting my efforts to go freelance as a computer programmer, taking on more than her share of chores and doing overtime in her job, as I chased work and established my business.

I shouldn't have got into it with Karen, I know.

I've always despised women who cheat, somehow it seems like a double betrayal when you are lesbians: solidarity of sisters and all that. Doing the dirty on the woman who is your partner and soulmate, just for the sake of sex, seemed morally wrong.

Just goes to show, you shouldn't take the moral high ground about anything, as you never know when you might find yourself in that lonely, windswept place. But with Karen, well, it was like a drug: I simply couldn't get enough of her.

We first locked eyes at a meeting with clients. "How do you take your coffee?" she asked, her blonde hair falling forward as she offered me a cup. "In bed with you", was my instant thought, but of course I said: "black, two sugars". During the meeting, I was totally distracted by her presence and could almost feel the sparks flying between us across the room. She coolly took notes as I stumbled through my presentation. I didn't deserve to get the contract, but somehow I convinced them my ideas were good.

Afterwards, I felt rather than saw her approaching me. 'A bit nervous, weren't you?' she said, smiling. 'Here's my personal number, if you want to go over anything with me.'

That was the start of it. I was besotted. We made love everywhere in her house: crushed onto the polished wooden floor, clothes flung around randomly as our bodies locked in desire. We stopped eating in the middle of meals, unable to wait any longer. The sex was sensational, she was so fit, eager and uninhibited. She twined around me, soaking, satiated. We made love in the shower, soaping each other, rinsing off, then starting over again, touching each other, groaning, moving naked and damp to the bed, her hair dripping sleek and wet onto my face, down onto my breasts, lower... I just couldn't get enough of her. She pounded in my brain, my loins were on fire, twitching, moistening at the thought of her. I could scarcely concentrate at work.

In my sane moments, I used to wonder why Wendy didn't spot what was happening. Once or twice, when I made one of my excuses to get away in the evenings, she looked at me with faintly narrowed eyes, but never questioned me. She just loaded the dishwasher and headed off to her Pilates class or the gym.

I felt like what I was – a heel.

'How do you keep looking so gorgeously slim?' I asked Karen one night. I was propped up in her bed, eating some peanuts as I watched her get dressed. There wasn't an extra ounce of fat on her, yet she seemed to eat the same as I did.

'Oh, lots of exercise and slimming meals when you aren't here,' she laughed, buttoning up her silk shirt.

Who knows how it would have ended if I hadn't had to go to Karen's flat unexpectedly one afternoon to collect some papers I'd accidentally left there a couple of nights before. I let myself quietly in with the key she'd given me some weeks before. Karen sometimes worked late into the night if her firm was particularly busy, and I didn't want to waken her if she was still sleeping.

I crept into the living room and picked up my pile of papers and turned to leave when a noise from the bedroom made me pause. There was just no mistaking the sound of sex. I flung open the bedroom door and watched the confusion of sheets and bodies condense into two shocked faces staring at me. Karen's face was ashen.
'What's going on here?' I shouted, the words thick in my mouth.
'Sorry Jo,' she said, her lip trembling. 'I was going to tell you about Gina, but could never find the words. I didn't want to hurt you!"
"I'll wait in the sitting room," I said, my angry tears choking my voice.

After a few minutes, I heard the front door open and close, then a nearby car start up. Gina had left, presumably. Karen, a robe tied round her, came into the sitting room and took a chair across from me.
'But, why? 'I asked when the words finally came.

Karen could scarcely meet my eye. "I'm sorry, Jo. This just isn't working between us. You're not free to be with me…there's Wendy… and besides, I've fallen for Gina. She's just everything I want, and she wants to be with me, too."

We talked back and forth, me angry, Karen apologetic at first, but becoming irritated and defensive.

Then she flung the final, devastating insult: "You're boring, Jo! And, and… I just don't want you anymore!"

With what dignity I could muster, I left Karen's house for the final time, flinging her house key down on the coffee table and slamming the door hard on my way out. It was a tiny satisfaction to hear the faint crash of an ornament falling from the shelf in the hall and smashing on the tiled floor.

You'd have thought Karen would have been delighted that I'd left without any more harsh words between us, and got on with her new life with Gina, but it didn't work out like that. I heard through the lesbian grapevine that a few weeks later, Gina had dumped Karen for a fitness instructor at her gym. Shortly after that, Karen began phoning me at work, begging me to take her back, and apologising for everything she'd said and done. This was before the days of mobile phones and emails being commonplace, so letters began to arrive at my workplace, increasingly angry in tone with threats of telling Wendy if I didn't resume the relationship.

I eventually agreed to meet her in a bar one evening.

"You have to leave me alone, Karen." My tone was cold and matter-of-fact. "We're done, it's over, and you made it very clear what you really think of me. It was fun while it lasted, but I'll never leave Wendy for you. I'm sorry it didn't work out for you with Gina, but someone else will come along for you. You're a good looking woman with a lot to offer the right person."

"But it's you I want, Jo! Gina was just a fling, please forgive me and let's get back to how we were!'

No amount of reasoning worked, so in the end I had to be harsh.

"No more letters, no more phone calls, nothing, Karen!" I burst out angrily. "Just leave me alone, now and always. I want nothing more to do with you."

Karen wiped her eyes and looked at me coldly.

"You utter bitch, Jo. Don't think this is the end of the matter, because it isn't! You used me for sex, took what you wanted and now you've had your fill of me, you're going back to the safety of wee wife and your fucking, boring life together! Was it just too much like hard work to leave her for me, to give up your comfort zone? Well, hell mend you, lady, this isn't over!"

Knowing that sometimes there's just no point in arguing or reasoning with someone in a rage, and there was nothing to be gained from reminding Karen that she had wanted me as much as I wanted her, or that she'd cheated on me with Gina, I simply threw some money on the bar counter and walked away, feeling guilty all over again about how I'd behaved towards Wendy. Adding to the guilt was a strong, gut feeling of unease and fear as to what Karen might do in the way of revenge. A woman scorned and spurned is a deadly creature...

The days turned into weeks, then months, and nothing happened. The letters and phone calls finally stopped, and I began to relax a little. Wendy suspected nothing, I was sure, and apart from her over-reaction to Shula's death, there appeared to be nothing amiss. Wendy made no comments as I began eating properly again and my weight returned to normal, except to say one night that I suited losing a few pounds. My feelings of guilt and shame gradually faded with time, although they never quite disappeared.

One evening as we sat by the fire, I studied Wendy as she sat mending one of my shirts. The needle glinted in the pool of light from the lamp, as she deftly and neatly sewed up a tear. This was the woman I really, truly loved. She was a decent person, lovely inside and outside, caring and kindly.

"You know that I love you, don't you?" My words, which came unbidden from my mouth, hung in the air, hovering, and waiting. Wendy paused in her sewing, and looked across at me. "Of course I know that, Jo," she said quietly. "Just as you know I love you, with all my heart."

"I'll put the kettle on. Tea?" I broke the tension and rose, heading for the kitchen. Maybe sometimes saying less is more...

***

"What a fool I was to risk what I had with Wendy, a kind, lovely and honest woman who adored me, all for the chance of cheap sex with a cheap, faithless woman!" Jo addressed the whisky decanter, which sat near her now, on the floor. "And all that time, she knew. I hurt her so badly, yet she still kept on loving me! If she'd thrown me out, it would have been just what I deserved, but she didn't! And now she's gone, and I can't even tell her how sorry I am to have done that to her."

She abandoned the packing and staggered back to bed, where she suffered a troubled, nightmare-laced sleep, waking around midnight with a crippling headache and dreadful thirst.

Chapter 7
Maureen McPhail

Maureen McPhail woke at 6.30 am without the aid of the alarm clock, a throwback to nursing days when her body clock was attuned to early rises. Sipping her cup of green tea, she mentally ticked off the chores for the day.

"First things first," she muttered. "Shower, breakfast, strip the bed and do the last minute packing." Alone for most of her adult life, Maureen often thought out loud these days, to fill the bleak silences and empty hours.

"So different from my nursing days," she mused, buttering some toast as Radio 4 news burbled on the kitchen radio, talking of the increasing levels of assaults on hospital staff. "Matron ruled the roost and any nonsense from patients or visitors simply wasn't tolerated!"

Ah, such happy days, she recalled. Training at Edinburgh's Royal Infirmary, she learned new skills every day, enjoying the contact with patients and the camaraderie of the other young women in the nurses' home, where they shared secrets and lipsticks in the evenings.

Matron had been a strict but fair boss, caring for the welfare of the young girls in her charge, but making sure they didn't breach the rules.

"I wonder whatever happened to Jessie McLeod?" Maureen mused, suddenly remembering a long-ago fellow student nurse. Jessie had sneaked out of the nurses' home one night to meet her boyfriend – how she'd got past the security man they never found out – but had been caught returning in the early hours of the following morning, trying to climb in the window of a ground floor bathroom.

Her short and tearful interview that day with Matron ended her embryo nursing career. Next day, Jessie was on the train from Waverley back to Oban, followed by a sad ferry passage to her parents' home on the Isle of Skye.

Maureen smiled wistfully, remembering those far off days when life was generally carefree and her biggest concerns were if her cap was on straight before the Ward Sister's inspection, or if her tiny salary would stretch to a visit to the cinema that week.

Suddenly, Maureen stiffened and her hand shook, allowing the tea in her cup to slop over into the saucer. Her memory had wandered, unbidden, to the next, awful chapter of her life at the hospital in Aberdeen. At first, it was wonderful, with an interesting new job, then the ecstasy of the romance, made all the more exciting because it was forbidden and had to be carried out in secrecy. She recalled so vividly all those scribbled notes slipped into her hand, the 'accidental' meetings in an empty side-ward, the trysts at coffee shops or dingy pubs far away from the hospital and the rare, or so rare! nights together in a back street hotel.

She had thrown away the cheap Woolworth's ring after it ended, flung it into Aberdeen harbour one dismal, cold night, her stomach churning and eyes glazed with tears as she struggled with the disbelief of betrayal. As she watched the dark waves moving as they quickly closed over the brass ring, she had, for a few minutes, considered flinging herself off the harbour wall and into the water, so ending all the pain. After all they'd been to each other, after what she'd helped him do to save his career… he had just abandoned her without a second thought.

"Thrown under the bus is today's expression," she said grimly to the empty kitchen, her voice echoing amongst the bare shelves and empty cupboards. "Well, it's all ancient history now," she added, gathering up the last of the dishes, "and I expect he's long dead now."

Her mind pulled up short there, trained over decades not to go any further or to pass through the iron gate into that cul-de-sac of memory. There was a no-go area beyond the gate, which was chained and padlocked, and the black box sitting beyond, in that dark, sad place, was clamped down shut with bands of steel. One false move, one sortie into that room would undo everything she's striven to blot out and she'd be back in that bleak, dark place she fought so hard to leave, all those years ago.

Sometimes, though, when acquaintances talked of their children and grandchildren, she couldn't help but wonder how it would have been if she'd had the baby and brought it up herself. Impossible! She knew there would be no support or help from the baby's father, or from her own family. She would be ostracised, shamed and blamed. Her nursing career's upward path would be, at best, stalled for years and at worst, ended entirely.

The termination, fortunately carried out legally in the late nineteen sixties, in a hospital distant from where she worked, had ended more than the baby's life, though. It took her away from the comfort and consolation of the Catholic Church. She'd never again set foot in a church, spoken with a priest or even communed privately with God, in whose eyes she knew she'd sinned. She was in self-imposed exile, cut off from her faith and her church.

Maureen ran a comb through her short grey hair, pausing only for a moment to meet her own eyes in the bathroom mirror, the only one not already carefully bubble wrapped and packed up in one of the dozens of sturdy cartons piled in the hall.

"Time for a new start, a new beginning, in a different place, where nobody knows me or anything about my past," she told herself. "Time to meet new people, have a little garden and live out my days in peace!"

"Ah, but the memories can't stay behind here in Edinburgh, in this flat, with the new owners", whispered a little voice in her head. "They'll go with you to Barleyknowe. You'll always remember, it's impossible to forget, impossible to forgive yourself. You'll always have that sick feeling in your stomach when you think about that night on the ward, his pleading with you early the next morning when the old lady was found dead in her bed, how he convinced you to counter- sign the new, falsified drugs dosage records to cover up the mistake, how together you destroyed the original, damning paperwork. So easy a mistake to make, 80 units of insulin on the chart instead of 8u, his poor handwriting making that fateful u almost closed to look like a zero. You'll remember that the night was frantically busy, and how you administered the drug almost on autopilot, you were so tired, distracted, thinking about him. The junior nurse with you didn't query the dosage, in fact, she hadn't really been paying attention, so anxious was she to get off shift and home, to put the gruelling day behind her."

The inner voice, incessant, clamouring now, insistent, carried on remorselessly.

"You'll remember his bland insincerity with the bewildered, grieving family in the morning, who knew their mother was very ill but thought she'd turned a corner.

"You'll remember how plausible he was, going into technical details about the underlying problems caused by diabetes and how they made the person susceptible to stroke and heart attack, how he consoled the family, pointed out their mother's advanced age and history of cardiovascular disease, and saying she would have passed away very peacefully in her sleep.

"You'll remember his abrupt cooling off, how he distanced himself from you, 'ghosting' they call it these days, then his sudden move back to his home area, to a hospital in Manchester for 'family reasons', so that his children could start school under the English system and so they could live nearer to his in-laws who helped out with childcare while he and his wife worked. All very plausible, but not the real reason for the move.

"You'll remember the desperate guilt and aching loss which consumed you for the months and years to follow, and you'll always remember the other thing, the lost child, however hard you try…"

Maureen slowly turned from the mirror's image of an old, sad woman, with bitterness etched round her eyes and thin lips set hard and unforgiving, and picked up her neatly typed list of tasks for her final night in the flat which had been her home for forty years. She'd miss the bustle of Edinburgh, the handy access to theatres, cinemas and restaurants, the vibrancy of the annual Festival and the calm greenness of the Botanic Gardens or the city's many parks.

"I won't miss my friends, though, because I have none!" The sour, angry thought strode into her head, unbidden. "You have no friends because you've always kept everyone at arm's length. You have mere acquaintances, women to share a trip to the theatre or opera, and that's how you've always wanted it to be!" she told herself briskly. "Your choice, Maureen! You could have a husband, children, good friends and confidantes. You picked this life of detachment, where nobody gets close, and where nobody can ever hurt you again!"

Her shoulders slumped as she thought of what had passed her by, and why. Then she straightened up, a distant memory of Matron's voice saying: "Stand up straight, girls! Shoulders back, best foot forward, and we'll have a friendly smile on those faces for the waiting patients, if you please! Now, I want to see a good day's work from all of you, and I'll be checking on how neatly those beds have been made, so no slipshod work. Go to it!"

Chapter 8
Frankie Anderson

Frankie scrabbled frantically amongst an unstable pile of books, papers, music scores, a half-eaten banana, and half a dozen tubes of paint – some oozing onto the kitchen table's oilcloth cover. Junk mail and fliers for Edinburgh Festival Fringe littered the surrounding chairs.

"Ah, here it is!" She grabbed the estate agent's brochure just before it slid onto the floor and into the pile of dirty clothes lying in front of the washing machine.

Running a hand through her unruly chestnut curls, she punched in the number on the brochure.

"Hi! Frankie Anderson here again: as you know I'm very interested in buying one of the cottages you're selling in Angus: Barleyknowe, near Forfar, and I now have the funds available to proceed, assuming the price is the same. Good, still fixed price, that's fine. I'd like a second look at the cottage I've chosen, before the formal offer from my lawyer. Yes, that's fine, email me a time and I'll meet you there on Tuesday. That's great, ta!"

She ended the call to the estate agent, pushed a jacket and bag onto the floor and flung herself down heavily on the cleared chair seat and began to cry, loud, gulping sobs which caused Misty to look up from her cat basket.

"Oh, Auntie Annie, how much do I miss you!" she wailed. "It feels so wrong to be happy at the thought of getting my own place at last, and you not here to share it all with me! But I wouldn't be able to do it if you hadn't left me all that money…oh, I wish you were here right now!"

Misty curled back up again in her basket and promptly fell asleep again. She was used to Frankie's ways: with her artistic temperament came sweeping highs and lows, an unpredictable life style and much emotion. Frankie wiped her eyes and rose from the table, and put the kettle on to boil. Auntie Annie would be glad that her favourite niece would at last have some security, and a home of her own, but it had come at such a cost, her sudden and quite unexpected death from a massive heart attack in, of all places, her favourite book shop. The shop's staff and then the paramedics did all they could to save her, but without success.

"Everyone told me she wouldn't have suffered," thought Frankie, tears springing to her eyes again, "but I never had a chance to say goodbye, to tell her how much I loved her!

She put a teabag to steep in a huge mug saying Old Train Drivers Don't Die, They Just Run Out Of Steam, wiped her eyes again and let her gaze wander round the detritus of the kitchen. "Guess I'll need to clean this place up before Johnny gets back," she muttered, then smiled at the thought of their reunion a few days ahead.

They'd met at art college, and had briefly been lovers, but had soon settled into the platonic friendship which suited them much better. After college, they rented a flat together and drifted along as months passed into years and they were now both in their mid-thirties. They had an easy, comfortable relationship, akin to the brothers and sisters they both lacked in real life, and were bonded by another, deeper coincidence. Both had been adopted as babies, Frankie by her aunt and Johnny by a childless couple. All Johnny knew was that his mother had been a young single woman with no support network and no choice but to have her baby adopted.

"One of these days I'll see if I can find my birth mother," Johnny had said one night when he and Frankie were talking about their families and lack of them. "I might wait till mum and dad pass away, though. They've been brilliant, loving parents and it might hurt their feelings if I go seeking out the woman who gave birth to me then gave me away."

"I get that, and being the lovely people they are, they'd probably encourage you to find your birth mother, but as you say, it might be hurtful for them if you found her and got to know her. It's a risk. " Frankie said after a moment's thought. "Sometimes it's best to let sleeping dogs lie."

Johnny was a designer with an advertising agency and Frankie as a computer programmer, but both were still passionate about their painting. They'd talked from time to time about buying a flat together, but never taken the idea further. They were happy as they were, with their easy companionship, as well as sharing the rent and the bills.

Frankie's gaze shifted to the blurred photograph in a beech wood frame, hung slightly askew on the wall above the table. It showed a teenage couple sitting on a wall, their heads thrown back in laughter at some joke, arms around each other and fingers entwined. "Just once. Just once I'd like to have met them, known them, talked with them, had a cuddle," Frankie said, looking at her parents with the usual sadness.

"They were different days then, Frankie," Aunt Annie had told her one day when they sat drinking wine in Annie's flat. "Your mum was only 15 when she got pregnant with you and Angus, your dad, wasn't much older at 16. There was actually police involvement because Tracy was under-age, and Angus was up on a charge of having sex with a minor: it was statutory rape, even though everyone knew they were just a young couple in love. My parents, your gran and grandad were just beside themselves when they found out she was pregnant, and quite out of their depth to deal with the situation. Tracy had been a late and unexpected baby for them. She was my lovely wee sister but 15 years younger than me, and they could scarcely cope with her, let alone the new baby she was carrying.

"He was a bit of free spirit, Angus," she said, smiling wistfully. "Whether he would have settled to being a dad and eventually a husband, we'll never know…" she tailed off as they both thought of the young man, emboldened by a few pints of beer, his reckless, helmetless motorbike ride through the dark, rainy night and the fatal collision with the tree, leaving his pregnant girlfriend distraught and inconsolable.

Frankie rose from her chair and moved closer to the photograph, studying the image of the woman who had given birth to her thirty five years earlier. Tracy's intractable depression following the trauma of Angus's death, the birth of a baby she failed to bond with, and her suicide at sixteen completed the absolute tragedy of Frankie's early life.

"There was talk of you going into care," Annie had eventually revealed to her then-teenage niece. "Gran and grandad were so heartbroken about Tracy's death – they seemed to age years overnight – and they simply weren't up to looking after an infant in any case. That's when I took you on!" she smiled. "And I've never regretted it for a minute," she laughed, ruffling her niece's mop of curls.
Annie was established in her career as an art teacher when Tracy died.

"But how did you know how to look after me?" Frankie asked her aunt, sitting on the kitchen table, her legs swinging in their ankle socks, biting into an apple with her perfect white teeth.

"Well, I didn't, Frankie! Luckily, I had some friends with babies, and with their help and some words of advice from the health visitor, and a little input from your gran, I somehow muddled through," her aunt laughed. "Someone gave me a copy of Dr Spock's Baby and Childcare book. One night, when you still wouldn't sleep at 3am and I'd done everything in the book to settle you, in desperation and with many apologies, I phoned my pal Marjorie, who had three children under five. She said: 'The problem is, sweetie, that Frankie hasn't read the book! Try some boiled, cooled water on a spoon. And then gin.' "Gin?" I'd shrieked, horrified. I'd heard about people giving their babies tiny amounts of whisky to make them sleep. In my befuddled state, I asked her if I should add ice, lemon and tonic water." 'No, you idiot!' Marjorie laughed. 'The gin's for you!'"

Frankie smiled at the memory of the conversation, and moved away from the photograph.

"Thank you, Auntie," she said to the room. "Thank you for everything you did for me and with me, for loving and encouraging me and for being my best friend."

Dashing away a tear, she began tidying up the kitchen.

Johnny would be home tomorrow and she wanted their last few days together to be harmonious. As she moved piles of old newspapers into a carrier bag for recycling, Frankie thought about their recent conversation.

The night she told Johnny of her plans to move away, possibly to the unusual living arrangement at Barleyknowe, he'd had run his hands through his floppy blond hair, in a gesture of bewilderment which was very endearing to his friends and his lovers.

Many a man and woman had had the sucker punch to the gut watching Johnny do just that. Did he do it deliberately? Frankie had often wondered if it was part of his seduction technique. It worked, anyway. Frankie had witnessed the stillness and concentration on the face of the other person about to succumb to Johnny's charms as he reeled them in with his open smile and cheery chat, his disarming manner and of course, his sensational good looks.

"It's not easy being bisexual, Frankie, is it?" he said one night as they lay cosy together on the settee, watching a movie on Netflix and eating popcorn. "When I'm with a bloke, it's great, but I miss the softness of a woman's skin, her lovely lips and her breasts. And when I'm with a woman, the maleness isn't there, the smell of a man, his rough cheek, his…"

"Ok, I know," Frankie laughed. "You don't need to spell it out. It's exactly the same for me, though I'm probably more on the lesbian than the bi side, if I had to choose."

"Not that I really have choices about this, I don't actually get to decide who I fall for, it just happens", she thought, holding Johnny's warm hand, feeling comfortable and safe with him. Counselling, following a very difficult break-up with an older boyfriend had established how needy she was, how much she craved affection, despite the unconditional love her aunt had lavished on her since her infancy.

"I just feel something is missing, there's never enough to fill up these gaps in me," Frankie had cried in the counselling session, her face tear streaked as gaps were filled, realisation and truth were uncovered.

"I have sex with people I don't love, just to feel needed and wanted for a couple of hours. I stuff food into my mouth, to fill the void, then I feel disgusted at myself and make myself sick. I drink too much, I smoke too much, anything to make me feel better, just for a short time. I hate myself, my lack of willpower and self-respect, and there's no-one to blame but me: nobody shoves food in my mouth or pours gin down my throat, or forces me to sleep with them: I could say thanks, but no thanks! What the hell is wrong with me?" she sobbed in the sessions.

"Knowledge is power, and self-awareness is the best knowledge to have," she'd confided to Johnny, after many counselling sessions and much agonising and reflection. "Doesn't stop you falling for unsuitable men and women, though, does it?" Johnny had said one night. "Mind you, I've no room to talk on that score," he added ruefully. "We're a right pair, aren't we?"

"But, why you going away up there, to Angus? We're happy here together in Edinburgh, aren't we?" Johnny said, when she told him of her plans.

His eyes were sad and downcast, and he looked, even more than usual, like a gorgeous puppy dog.

"I have to start making a different life, Johnny," she'd said, taking his hand in hers. "You know why. I need a fresh start after what happened with Marion…"

She bit her lip to keep the tears back. "I have to get right away, so there's no danger of bumping into her in the Filmhouse or John Lewis. It kills me to think of her back with her husband after what we were to each other, how could she dump me like that?" Her voice broke and she began to cry.

The tears were never far away, even though it was almost a year since Marion had ended their relationship. Dates with a couple of other women and one man since then had been nothing but sticking plasters on an open, unhealed wound.

She went through the motions, even sleeping with one woman, but ending up feeling worse instead of better. They weren't Marion, she with the warm brown eyes, the rich flick of hair, the perfect breasts and the pulse which throbbed hard in her neck when she climaxed, groaning, in Frankie's arms.

"I loved her so, so much," Frankie sobbed. "I'll never love anyone like that again, you know all this Johnny! You sat night after night with me, bless you, coaxing me to eat something, pleading with me not to drink anymore wine, cuddling up with me in bed just so I wouldn't be alone. You know how much I love you, how much you mean to me, you can visit as often as you like, but I have to leave Edinburgh. The city's poison to me now. I'm terrified I'll see her with her family in the museum, or on a tram… it's just unbearable!"

The tears ran down her face, unchecked.

"I see her everywhere anyway," she cried. "Every grey Volvo that passes by me could be hers, though she's probably changed her car by now anyway! I think it's her in front of me in Tesco, that beautiful shining hair falling as she stoops to take milk from a shelf. Then the woman turns, and it isn't Marion, and my heart drops like a stone. I see her a few feet ahead of me in Princes Street, I hurry past and glance back, but then it isn't her, of course, it's a stranger. I want to see Marion, and yet I don't want to see her. I remember every detail of how it was when we were together, how her hand felt in mine, her lovely eyes, the faint scent of her perfume and her beautiful smile. I've blocked seeing her posts on Facebook and Twitter, but still, I'm desperate to know what she's doing.

"Is she still with her husband, is there another woman in her life now, does she miss me, or am I just history, a forgotten dalliance which was just a bit of fun at the time? And then, I fall asleep, and she's in my dreams, but when I reach out to hold her, to touch her, to kiss her, she fades away."

She paused. Johnny said nothing, but continued to hold her close, gently stroking her hair.

"It's been a kind of madness, an unhealthy obsession, I know," she went on. "I wanted to know everything about her, see all her baby photos, the family snaps: if there had been a DVD of her whole life, I'd have watched it from the start: her first kiss, how she looked as a teenager, changing hairstyles, the music running through her head, the books she read, everything, everything… like some demented collector of stamps or butterflies, I wanted to gather every scrap of information about her, to fill in all the blanks, to know her inside out, to understand this beautiful woman that I loved so much."

Her face wet with fresh tears, Frankie turned to Johnny. "I know, it's insane how Marion filled my senses, my head and heart and even the spaces where I used to keep my common sense and intelligence. I wasn't in control, the world careered around me in sparkling, rainbow colours when I was with her, then it all turned black and sad when she went away from me again, back to her husband and her children and the life I couldn't be a part of…"

A little more calmly, but with a voice still laced and heavy with tears, Frankie continued.

"After Jeff and I broke up and I had the counselling, I really felt much better about myself, more in control, and not just doing what someone else wanted. You know that I was recovering! Then Marion comes along and messes with my head big-time, so I didn't know where I stood with her. She changed her mind, sometimes on a daily basis, till I didn't know if I was coming or going, was it on or was it off? She spent weeks, months deciding between me and her husband, and all the while I fell deeper in love with her.

" I've never felt like that about anyone before, she just consumed me! It's like having some horrible virus I just can't shake off, and I fear that I never will, life will just never be the same again. And now that Auntie Annie's passed away, it's like I'm grieving two huge losses at the same time."

Johnny waited a moment, then said quietly: "Marion fucked you over, Frankie. Her conflicts and confusion about her sexuality and her marriage spilled over onto you, so you became collateral damage. I don't think for a minute that she meant to hurt you this badly, she's basically a nice woman, but that's what happened.

" She had her safety and security, not to mention her comfortable home to go back to after her dalliances with you. It was never going to work for you, sweetie. Even if she'd taken that big step and left her husband, what would have happened about her children? It would have been constant conflict and guilt for her, whatever arrangement was sorted out. It would have driven you both mad in time. Your relationship simply wouldn't have been able to withstand the pressures and both your hearts would have been shattered. I'm not making excuses for her, sweetie, but she had an awful lot to lose, you know. "

As Frankie cried in his arms, soaking his shirt with her tears, he said:

"Someone else will come along in time for you, darling. Someone who'll help all this go away, and make you happy again." Johnny's voice was muffled by her sobs. "I just don't think you're likely to find someone in rural Angus, in an isolated commune set-up. You could be very lonely!"

Straightening up, Frankie blew her nose loudly on the wad of tissues he held out to her. "I'm done with all that!" Frankie exclaimed. "Women, and men, they're not worth all the grief and the hassle! Misty and I will be fine in our wee cottage with no temptations around, and my heart won't be broken again!"

Johnny held her tightly, then said softly: "Darling Frankie, you're a warm, bright, tactile, gorgeous woman, who lights up every room you enter. You've so much love and affection to give the right person, don't close down! Marion hurt you so much, and by the way, she must be feeling mega guilty for leading you on like she did, then dumping you! But not everyone is like Marion, or in Marion's situation, and you need to take some responsibility here too: you knew from the get-go that she was married with children. There's someone out there for you, someone uncomplicated and kind and loving, who'll return all your love without any holding back, without blowing hot and cold, playing mind games or messing with your head."

Frankie sniffed, listening.

"See, honey," Johnny continued, warming to his theme, "if you stand in front of a blazing fire, you'll get the warmth you need, but there's a chance you could be burned by a spark. If you stand back, out in the cold, there's no danger of you being hurt, but there's no warmth either. You're one of life's warm people, and you need the heat of that fire."

He stroked her mass of curls.

"Yes, you've been badly, horribly hurt by Marion, and it does feel like an illness, being rejected by someone you love deeply. But, I think the virus will leave you and you'll soon be at the recovery stage where you're lying on the sofa with a cosy blanket and a bottle of Lucozade. You'll get better, just give yourself a bit longer."

He hugged her again, and she snuggled into his arms.

"How about tonight we have a takeaway, a nice bottle of red and watch a movie, maybe Love, Actually again? It'll make you cry, I know, but maybe it'll be a different kind of crying. I think ET might be too much tonight, eh? I've seen your meltdowns when ET goes home at the end, I don't think my shirt could cope with any more drenchings!"

Frankie put her arms round him and hugged him tightly.
"You know that I love you, don't you?" she said. "I'm going to miss you like mad, and I want you to visit me loads, but this is something I have to do…"
Johnny pulled her close and kissed the top of her head, feeling her tensions lessening as she relaxed. The film rolled on, but his concentration waned. He thought about Frankie leaving, the giant hole it would create in his life.

"I love her so much," he thought, "but not in the way she needs to be loved. I just can't be that person for her, I'd always want to be with someone else, and chances are high that it would be with another bloke. Maybe this is for the best, having space between us. She needs to get away, find who she is, what she wants out of life, away from our cosy wee set up here, and maybe it's time I sorted myself out too and focused on where I'm going, instead of drifting along like this. There's the other thing too… do I want to go down that road, find out what happened, why my mother gave me up?"

"You're thinking about something, I can feel it!" Frankie exclaimed, shifting in his arms. "It'll be fine, Johnny, we won't lose our connection. Now, concentrate on the film, there's that good bit coming where Hugh Grant dances down the stairs at No 10!"

He hugged her and smiled. She was right, the connection was there, for good. She was the sister, the best pal, the soulmate he had found and they'd never really be apart.

***

Across the city of Edinburgh, a few miles from where Frankie and Johnny hugged in mutual companionship, in streets of douce sandstone terraced houses, lamps were being lit and curtains drawn against the winter evening. Here and there, lights shone in cheerful rooms before drapes had been pulled. Passers-by could glimpse domestic tableaux of people eating round a kitchen table, bowls of pasta steaming and teenagers with headphones ignoring the rest of their family. Dogs lay panting by blazing log fires, the pages of books were turned, ironing boards pulled open to deal with the laundry pile, and dishes stacked in draining racks.

In one such home, Marion sat on a low chair between the beds of her two young daughters, reading The Tiger Who Came to Tea. The book was well worn, and a favourite with the children, as it had been with Marion and her brother many years before.

As she read, mechanically putting expression into the familiar words, her mind slid away, as it did regularly, to Frankie, to the awfulness of their last meeting, the pain she'd seen consuming the younger woman's face when she told her it was over.

"Have you ever walked away from someone you loved?" The question had been part of a women's magazine quiz Marion had glanced at in the hairdressers recently. Yes, she had walked away in the end from the woman she loved so much, and her guts still knotted with guilt, sorrow and loss at the memory.

She knew that she had almost destroyed Frankie with her inability to make up her mind and her constantly blowing hot and cold over their relationship. The only decent thing she'd done, the only thing she could have done, to spare Frankie further pain, was to end it once and for all, to cut off all ties and never see her again. The pain was with her constantly, the sorrow and the guilt, and the dreadful, aching loss of the woman she had fallen for so hard, so completely and who she still loved. When she closed her eyes, all she saw was Frankie's smiling face framed by her mass of unruly hair.

"Mummy, why are you crying?" her younger daughter Lily sat up in bed and tugged at her sleeve, her eyes anxious.

"Och, it's just that sad bit when the tiger goes away again, Lily. Don't mind me, I'm just being a bit silly!"

In the other bed, Anna said nothing, but looked thoughtfully at her mother.

Downstairs in his study, Alistair stacked up his pile of marking ready to give out to his third year geography class the next day, and pushed the chair back from his desk. Through the door, which was slightly ajar, he heard the faint murmur as Marion read to their girls. Running his hand through his hair, Alistair wondered, not for the first time in the past few months, what was wrong with his wife. She'd stopped going out to her book club and meeting her friends for coffee, and there was a sadness hanging about her which was hard to fathom.

"Well, I did ask her," he thought, "and she said there was nothing wrong, so I can't fix something I don't understand. Maybe she just needs a break, a change of scene?"

Purposefully, he opened his computer and began searching on line for mini breaks in the next school holidays. The girls could go to their gran's in Troon for a few days, and he'd surprise Marion with a short holiday. York might be a good idea: or even Venice?

A relaxing break in a good hotel with meals she didn't need to cook might be just the thing to lift her mood, he thought, clicking through the holiday sites. And maybe their sex life would get back to normal as well. It seemed a long time since they'd made love with any real enthusiasm on her part. She let him take her body, that was all, really, it was as if she was on auto pilot, ticking the boxes, but not really there. He sensed too that she was faking an orgasm to get things over and done with, and that was a new and unwelcome thought. Alistair sighed.

He loved his wife and hated how distant and sad she was these days. He must try to make things right again.

***

In her flat, Frankie began washing a week's worth of dishes, glancing at the kitchen clock. Johnny would be back soon, and they'd have supper and a drink, and enjoy these last few weeks of living together.

"We'll miss him, won't we, Misty?" she asked the cat. "I can't leave you behind though. You're going to just love being a country cat: all those fields to run through, and mice to catch! I just hope I'm going to love being a country girl," she added, rinsing cold water over the plates. "We'll make it work, though, won't we? I'm determined to be a happier person, and put all of this behind me!"

Purposefully, she scrubbed pots, singing along to Radio 2 while Misty curled up in her basket and went back to sleep.

Chapter 9
New Homes

Glen View, No 1 Barleyknowe Cottages

The women all arrived over the course of a fortnight, as the Angus winter of 2010 continued to rage, throttling traffic and disrupting work patterns. Gritters and snowploughs battled through the long nights to keep the network of roads passable, the plough drivers watching in despair as fresh snow fall on the stretches they'd just cleared. The brief hours of daylight brought little improvement, and a weariness began to overtake the communities as they cleared paths and trudged on foot to the shops.

Rose and Irene were first to arrive after Jennifer, arriving in snow and battering wind to unlock the door of No 1 Barleyknowe cottages, which they'd named Glen View.

"It's a bit clichéd, but very accurate," said Irene when Rose suggested the name. Their new home had a good view of the rolling hills of the Angus Glens, which were coated in heavy, dense snow the day the couple hurried from a laden car into the haven of the cottage.

Like Jennifer had done in the farmhouse, their first task was to fire up the boiler, and turn up the heating to warm their new home. Rose also laid a fire in the sitting room wood burner, to add cosiness to the atmosphere. Used to the convenience of gas central heating in their Perth bungalow, the women had discussed the shift to oil-fired central heating from a tank and accepted a different way of budgeting for fuel at Barleyknowe.

"I'm putting on the kettle, you'll be pleased to hear!" Irene called through from the kitchen, as Rose closed the stove door, watching orange flames lick up the chimney.

An earlier text message to Rose from the furniture removal company confirmed what they feared: the van was stuck in slow-moving traffic caused by the drifting snow, and would be arriving a couple of hours later than they expected.

"Well, let's unpack the car and do what we can till the furniture arrives," she said. "No point fretting, they'll get here sometime. This is like the TS Eliot poem The Journey of the Magi, isn't it? Something about the wise men having a cold coming of it…" She trailed off as she saw the irritated expression on Irene's face.

"For god's sake, Rose, will you stop with these literary quotes and all this pretentious crap? You're a retired chemistry teacher, not a flipping literary critic for the Sunday Times!"

Rose flushed and turned away to hide her tears, and headed for the door to begin unloading their bags and boxes. She hauled out the first few bags with unnecessary force, while her thoughts tumbled around in a depressing, dark kaleidoscope of miserable images.

"When will Irene recognise and accept that I've more interests than just chemistry? I love hearing poetry, I love reading and hearing the written word, just as I love music, painting, nature and animals! So what if she despises reading, sees it as a waste of time, when she could be watching rugby or tramping around in the rain for miles!"

Rose dumped the cartons in the bare hallway and turned back out to the car for the next load, her cheeks whipped red by the biting, snow-laced wind. Her breath was rasping. "I hope I'm not going to have a go of my asthma," she thought, closing the boot and hurrying back inside.

"Maybe I should never have got together with her," the nagging voice in her head went on as she returned to the car for a final load. "Maybe George was right all those years ago, when he screamed at me I was making a big mistake leaving him and going off with her. And now there's this situation about Katherine and her family... when am I ever going to see my lovely grandchildren again, after what Irene said to them last Christmas?"

The awful shouting, those words which couldn't be taken back again, Irene's angry face, flushed after several glasses of wine, her bitter comments to Katherine and James about their neglect of Rose, her criticisms of their life style and the way they were raising their children had all tumbled out in a tipsy rush into the horrified stillness around the festive table. The ghastly silence was only broken when Iona began to cry quietly into her Santa napkin, and her mother moved to comfort the girl. The memory of that awful meal, and their strained, early departure on Boxing Day came back in sharp relief, hurting Rose, just as the icy breath of winter lashed her skin.

She pulled two more large bags out of the car and closed the boot. Enough for one day, the rest could wait until tomorrow.

Closing the sturdy door behind her, Rose noticed with a slight release of tension that Irene was quickly stuffing a hanky into her jumper sleeve. She'd obviously been crying.

Irene looked round and met Rose's gaze. They shared a long, still moment, then Irene opened her arms to her partner. "I'm so sorry, Rose," she said. "I really don't deserve you, do I?"

Rose said nothing, staring impassively at the woman she had loved for so many years.

"We'll make all this work," said Irene. "We can have a great life here, it's a fresh start, a new chance for us to be happy."

She studied Rose's face, and said, her voice trembling: "You know that I'm nothing without you, you're the better part of us, the grown-up, my rock, my life…" The tears began to flow again.

Rose folded Irene into her arms and rocked her gently.

"We've had a long day, we're both tired. Things will look better in the morning, after a good night's sleep. Let's have a cuppa and some food – I've brought the groceries in from the car- while we wait for the removal van, then we can put everything to rights in the morning."

The women stayed in the embrace for a minute or two longer, breathing in the familiar scents of each other's perfume and the fabric conditioner which softened their clothes. Rose stroked Irene's grey head, remembering for a second her partner's long gone, flame-coloured, beautiful hair.

A *coup de foudre*, lightning striking, a bolt from the blue…all those clichés had suddenly been true, the day they first met in the staffroom, Irene the chemistry teacher, newly arrived from another school to join Rose's department…

Rose broke off her musing, and gently disentangled herself from Irene.

"I think that might be the van arriving, I hear the noise of a heavy engine coming up the road."

The moment ended, as the two women bustled to clear a pathway for the removal men, and watch the stream of possessions enter their new home.

The cottage watched, and waited, its old timbers warming and creaking faintly as the new and very efficient wood burning stove flicked warmth and light into every corner of the cosy sitting room.

***
Marchmont, No 5 Barleyknowe Cottages

Maureen made the long drive from Edinburgh in what there was of winter daylight, and leaving the city early, made it to Angus by lunchtime. The sky was brittle blue, low sun glinting fiercely on the snow-laden fields and glens. She had to change to her prescription sunglasses for the last hour's drive, the reflective brightness dazzling her vision.

Drawing up outside her cottage, which she'd named Marchmont after her previous Edinburgh home area, she noted smoke drifting from the farmhouse and cottage number 1, almost directly across from her.

"At least I'm not here first," she thought, unlocking the door of her new home and, as Irene and Rose had done, going straight to the boiler controls to begin heating up the rooms. A short time later, her removal van arrived and the men began unloading cartons and furniture, rugs and lamp standards.

With her usual efficiency, Maureen had labelled each carton with a coloured sticker, so very soon the boxes were sitting in the correct rooms, silent, and waiting to be unpacked. Tipping the men and closing her front door, Maureen spotted a figure at the window of the cottage across from hers. "Rose or Irene, I didn't get a proper look, but no doubt I'll see them before too long," she thought, plugging in the radio, and then filling the kettle.

"First things first, a cup of tea, then down to work!" This she spoke out loud, almost as an encouragement to her tired body. The drive had been stressful, with snow showers alternating with sleet and brighter spells, and she felt drained and weary, and suddenly a little afraid and apprehensive. What was she doing, leaving behind Edinburgh, a city she loved, to come up here where she knew no-one? No more popping to Jenner's for afternoon tea, or going to see an arthouse movie at the Filmhouse, just to break the crushing loneliness of her solitary life, just to get away from the four walls of her flat, the silence broken only by the ticking of the clock she was gifted on her retirement.

"Right, lady, this'll not do one bit," she told herself firmly, the alter ego taking over, as it did from time to time. "We're not going to head down this road, are we? You've had a stressful, long and very tiring day. Let's get the bed made up, the microwave unpacked, then supper and an early bed for you, complete with hot water bottle!"

***

The Old Dairy, No 4 Barleyknowe Cottages

Jo's arrival later that week was dramatic, as she skidded on an icy pothole, while driving along the farm road to Barleyknowe, coming to a halt against a solid and unforgiving fence post. The bumper was badly dented and a wing mirror was broken, but from what she could see, everything else on the Datsun was unscathed.

Maureen had been outside her cottage, clearing snow, when she heard the bang a couple of hundred yards away, and she ran down to help her new neighbour.

"It doesn't look too bad," said Jo, as Maureen hurried towards her. "Just a damn nuisance!" She drove slowly to The Old Dairy, emptied the contents into the house, and then stowed the injured car away from the courtyard, in the communal car park behind the barns.

"I'll ring the garage to tow it into Forfar," Jo told Maureen over a cup of coffee in Marchmont a few minutes later, "just in case there's other damage I can't see."

Shortly afterwards, Jo thanked her neighbour for the hot drink, and excused herself. "My furniture isn't arriving until tomorrow, but I've things to organise today, including the car repair now!"

Maureen hummed under her breath as she loaded the coffee cups and her breakfast things into the dishwasher, and glancing at the mirror in the kitchen, was surprised to see herself smiling.

***

Meadowfields, No 2 Barleyknowe Cottages

Frankie, driving her red mini and followed up the farm road by a transit van, pulled up at Meadowfields during a brief thaw in the weather. The road surface glistened still with the threat of frost, but there was a softening of the banked up snow at the sides of the road. The driver of the van, and another man, helped her unload, what seemed to her watching neighbours, very few possessions into her cottage. The whole operation took only an hour, including Frankie unpacking the mini and carefully carrying Misty in her cat carrier into the cottage. The door shut firmly, the white van did a careful U-turn in the courtyard, and silence descended again.

Behind the door, Frankie attended to the cat's needs first, putting down food and water and filling a litter tray. "There, sweetheart, this is home for us now."

The cat stalked slowly around the cottage, going from room to room and finally settling in the kitchen, winding herself around Frankie's legs, then curling up in her familiar basket.

Frankie stopped unpacking dishes to answer a text from Johnny, asking if she's arrived safely. "Yep, we're just settling in," she replied. "I'll do the unpacking tomorrow, but right now I'm too knackered to do anything! Yes, I miss you too, loads, already."

Misty settled herself for sleep, listening to her mistress chat and hearing the deeper, fainter noises of the ancient stones of the cottage, the whispers of previous people and animals, the old laughter and tears, singing and shouting which had sunk into the walls.

Chapter 10
Horseshoes Is Occupied

The rental cottage lay empty for a month or so after all the other women moved in to their houses and began turning them into homes. One of the pair of cottages which had previously been an old stable block, 7 Barleyknowe Farm Cottages, named Horseshoes by Jennifer, sat silent, its blank windows staring into the courtyard, observing the daily movements of its neighbours. For those with ears to hear, the faintest whinny and clatter of hooves leached from its walls from time to time as the generations of ghost horses moved around, and for everyone else, the wind was whistling and making odd noises…

The first snowdrops, planted years before by the farmhands who had lived in the cottages at Barleyknowe, had already forced their way bravely through the bitter, snow shrouded earth and died off again before the cottage finally had an occupant.

The first occupant of Horseshoes was spotted a few weeks after the others had settled into their new homes. Freya arrived in a flurry of early spring rain, her ancient Volvo pulling noisily to a halt outside number seven, narrowly missing a cluster of miniature daffodils in the strip of garden outside the house.

Irene was cleaning the insides of the windows of their cottage and had a good view of their new, temporary neighbour as she lugged numerous cases, boxes, bags and a tapestry weaving loom indoors.

"Come and see this," she called to Rose. "The new person's brought everything but the kitchen sink with her!" Rose turned down the heat on the soup she was making and joined her partner at the window. The two women, standing discreetly back from view, watched for a few minutes as their new neighbour flurried between the car and the house, often dropping items on the way and muttering to herself as she did so. Smiling, Irene resumed polishing the windows. "She looks like a character, it'll be interesting getting to know her."

"We'll have her over for coffee once she's settled in," Rose called from the kitchen, as she added some seasoning to the lentil soup.

Freya's arrival had been noticed by all the women except Elaine, who still went to Dundee some days to check on the running of her businesses. She didn't meet Freya until the weekend, when they literally bumped into each other in the courtyard.

Elaine was walking head down, shrouded against the rain by a hooded rain coat, towards the car park behind the barns, when she almost collided with Freya, who was similarly dressed and heading purposefully towards Jennifer's house.

"Oh, I'm sorry!" they both said at once, then exchanged a few words about the awful weather.

"I'm just heading to Jennifer's with these letters which have arrived: I think they're to do with council tax or something for the cottage I'm renting," said Freya earnestly. "Doesn't do to let these official things drift, does it? *Ne dissimulatione postponere*!"

Elaine held back a smile and hurried on towards her car, where she'd left some business paperwork.

"You see it all, you absolutely do!" she thought wryly, hurrying back to the warmth and peace of her home. Just as well she was accustomed to dealing with eccentric elderly ladies who visited her salons…

Gradually, all the women met Freya, who invited them round for herbal tea and to see the cottage, which, although fully modernised, still retained some features of its history as a stable.

"You see, they've kept that door which is split in two halves with the distinctive sneck lock," she instructed Irene and Rose, pouring out very strong tea into two oddly-shaped earthenware and none-too-clean mugs. "Very typical of rural architecture in the 19th and early 20th century. Irene dared not meet Rose's eye for fear of exploding with laughter, and instead asked what Freya did for a living.

"Oh gosh, I retired eons ago," said Freya. "I was a classics teacher, but now I have time to write poetry and to finally concentrate on my magnum opus on the lives of the suffragettes. It's an Iliad-style epic poem, you know, and I had to get away from the bustle and demands of my life in Bearsden to concentrate properly!"

The sleeve of Freya's kaftan brushed the precarious mountain of jam-laden scones she'd piled onto a plate, and Rose moved swiftly to stop the whole lot falling to the floor.

"Oh, thank you," said Freya, "this cottage is so small I'm always bumping into things and knocking them over. Now, would you like to see my tapestry? It's not coming along too well, I unpick a lot of mistakes each morning. Like Penelope, you know, warding off suitors as she waited for Odysseus to return!"

Irene covered her unbidden snort of laughter with a hasty cough, and Rose swiftly changed the subject to the safe topic of the weather and the fierce winds which were battering the north east of the country at the time.

Once in the safety of their own home, as Rose feared, Irene let rip, her caustic wit targeting the absent Freya. Why did she have to be so cruel? Rose wondered for the umpteenth time what pleasure it gave her partner to be so scathing about everyone, to find and magnify their faults and foibles. She sighed inwardly.

"I bet that's not even her real name!" Irene began. "I expect she's called Jean or Doris and she's chosen Freya to make her sound different and interesting! It's like she's assembled all the stereotypes going and lumped them together into her person. All those velvets, beads, floaty kaftans, incense sticks, weird food and no doubt homemade wine, concocted from something very obscure and tasteless, piled together into a gigantic, tedious old woman!"

The true reality of Freya's life was exposed when Rose dropped by with a jar of homemade jam for the temporary resident.

Her name was not Freya, as Irene had guessed. Several envelopes lying in view on the cluttered table were addressed to Ms Margaret Jackson, and there was in evidence a jigsaw of Downton Abbey, which had been covered with a large tea towel when she and Irene had visited. The famous tapestry was still at an early stage and the only signs of any writing were a couple of pages of scribbled notes sitting on top of a copy of the Woman's Own.

Rose took her leave of Freya, turning down the offer of a cup of herbal tea.

"I won't mention to Irene what I've discovered," she mused, crossing the courtyard to her own cottage. "It'll just encourage her to make more nasty comments. We're all entitled to our deceptions, especially when we get on in years a bit!"

Days turned into weeks, then weeks to months. The women formed loose friendships, met for coffee and chat and organised the occasional communal meal in the barn, but largely led their own lives through the winter months.

The spring brought kinder weather, and as the months moved towards summertime, the community spirit began to flourish.

Jennifer, alone in the farmhouse, worked in a study which had windows at either end of the room. Her desk sat at the window overlooking the courtyard, but now and then she'd take up a seat on a velvet covered sofa at the rear window, which had a view of the field she owned, and an outlook to the Angus Glens.

She observed the comings and goings, and the way the women interacted, noticing their body language and sometimes hearing snatches of conversation on the sunnier days when the windows were open to let the house air.

Secretly, she noted Rose's unhappy face, Irene's barely suppressed and almost chronic expression of anger and the over-full bottle recycling container at their back door.

She observed Frankie's over-the-top cheerfulness, obviously covering up something darker. "What a beautiful woman she is," mused Jennifer, watching Frankie cleaning the windows of Meadowfields one day. The younger woman was dressed in faded jeans and an old t-shirt spattered with traces of paint and her curly hair was pulled back with a scrunchie. Frankie hopped up and down on the step ladder, polishing the glass, her top riding up a little as she stretched her arm to reach the top pane. A tiny strip of flesh showed between the waistband of her jeans and the t-shirt, making the watching Jennifer catch her breath and turn away from the window. "I'll bet she hasn't a clue how attractive she is, with that gorgeous smile, fantastic figure and her fabulous, funny ways," said Jennifer to herself, sitting down to work. "This won't do, you know," she told herself, sternly. "You're just not going there!"

Jennifer had also noted Maureen's closed-off demeanour and stand-offishness, staying just this side of polite with most people, although she seemed to thaw a little in Jo's presence.

"Jo's a good person," thought Jennifer, as they all sat round a trestle table in the barn one Sunday afternoon after one of their occasional communal meals. The pot luck lunch that day had been good fun, with everyone bringing a dish and drinks.

Jo had been on good form that day, telling silly jokes and anecdotes, mostly against herself, and successfully drawing the more reticent women like Elaine and Maureen into the conversation.

The one woman mostly eluding Jennifer's scrutiny was Elaine, who spent several days a week in Dundee, and appeared to be often away in the evenings, returning late at night. Elaine was polite and even friendly with the other women, but there was a reticence, a closed-offness about her too.

Unable to sleep one night, as was always the case when the date came round each year, Jennifer sat in the dark at her bedroom window, which also overlooked the courtyard. She saw the ghostly flap of a barn owl's wings as it swooped down onto its prey in the field, and was gazing into the black velvet of the sky, studded with stars, when she heard the faint sound of a car making its way slowly up the track.

Elaine's car came into view and then disappeared as it was driven into the communal car park behind the barns. Jennifer heard the engine cut, and a second later saw Elaine walk swiftly towards Springburn cottage. At her side was a man Jennifer vaguely recognised but couldn't quite place. Interesting, she thought, returning to her bed. Very interesting.

Throughout the spring and summer of 2010, the residents of Barleyknowe cultivated the solitary field which Jennifer had purchased along with the buildings. She'd supplied a fully-equipped tool shed, two greenhouses, fruit cages and starters for all the fruit and vegetable plants, but encouraged the women to introduce other ideas.

"Maybe we should get a couple of beehives?" said Jo to Maureen one summer's day as they watered tomatoes and sweet peppers in the greenhouses. The air was humid and dense and the automatic openers on the greenhouse panes had released several hours beforehand. A stray butterfly landed on the tomato plants before escaping out again into the clean beauty of the Angus air.

"Good idea," said Maureen, watering lettuce seedlings which would soon be ready to plant out.

"Time for a break, eh?" said Jo, opening the greenhouse door. In the field, Frankie and Irene were staking up runner beans while in the fruit cages, Rose weeded the rows of strawberries.

Elaine, on a day off work, appeared with a huge jug of lemonade and half a dozen glasses. The women sat to drink, and were discussing plans for the winter crops they intended to plant later, when Freya joined them.

"When is it you leave us, Freya?" said Maureen, pleasantly.

"Oh, a few weeks yet," the woman replied.

"When the autumn mists begin to form, I'll set off home again and my rural interlude will end!"

"About September, then?" said Jo, suppressing a smile.

"Ah, yes, as the leaves begin to turn in a dying fall!" Freya exclaimed.

"Jeezo," thought Frankie. "This woman's truly bonkers", but she simply smiled sweetly and offered the eccentric old woman a glass of lemonade.

"Oh, well, just this once, I'll risk non-organic," trilled Freya.

Elaine looked up at the sky and away from anyone's gaze. She didn't trust herself not to laugh out loud, and that would be so rude…

Jennifer, standing back a little from her open rear window, smiled at the scene below her.

That evening, Facetiming her old friend Maria in London, she recounted a couple of tales of the doings of the women.

To her surprise, the friend reacted badly.

"Jennifer, you're such a fucking control freak. You're like some horrible puppet mistress, manipulating these women, getting them to work your bloody field, spying on them, mocking them and laughing at their quirky ways! We've all got our foibles, you and me included, but they aren't all of what makes us who and what we are! When are you going to engage properly with life again, get down and dirty, let somebody in and stop living vicariously?"

Shocked, Jennifer was silent for a moment, unprepared for this attack and absorbing what her friend had just said. She replied slowly. "I like all these women but it's true, sometimes I do feel like the detached outsider, as if I'm watching a movie. I'm not really connecting with them properly, and I don't think it's because I'm the major owner here. I stopped the therapy sessions when I left London and was hoping not to need them again, much was dealt with as you know, but maybe a bit of counselling would help me to get further down the road. As for getting down and dirty with anyone, you know what happened with Vanessa, I simply can't do all that again!"

Maria's tone softened. "I'm sorry, Jen, that was harsh of me. I know as well as anyone what you've been through, but you've changed your mobile number, your email address and even where you live. You've blocked Vanessa on all your social media accounts, nothing remains, and she's history, Jennifer! She can't touch you, hurt or damage you ever again. Of course you won't forget her completely, or what happened, you literally bear the scars, I know that, you had a terrible time, my god, having to phone the police, and the spell in the Women's Aid shelter, we were all horrified, but it's all gone, past, away! Jennifer, you need to break out of that icy shell you're in and start connecting properly again! You're a strong woman, look what you've achieved in your life so far, and there's much to go still. "And as for the other thing, you'll never forget that either but maybe it's time you stopped beating yourself up over it! How many years is it now?

"He'll be 35 now..." Jennifer tailed off, feeling her throat constrict. "I hear what you're saying, Maria, I get it, I know you've my interests at heart, but I don't want to talk anymore tonight. Catch you again soon." Abruptly, she ended the call and sat for a long time, before eventually rising slowly and going to the kitchen to put the kettle on. Suddenly, she felt decades older than her 50 years. Old, weary, very sad, and disgusted with herself. Maria was right, this wasn't some huge game. These were real people, with real feelings. It was time to change, to put the past where it belonged and to start engaging properly with life again. No more of this gazing in from the outside, like some sad child with its nose pressed to life's window. She wanted the warmth of someone's love, a woman's loving arms around her, someone to talk to after the solitude of a day at her laptop, someone to cook alongside, laugh and cry with, make love with…

She wanted Frankie.

***

At the end of Freya's six month tenancy, the women gave her a farewell party in the communal barn, bringing food and drink and decorating the trestle table. Frankie played guitar, and Freya read some of her poetry, which turned out to be both rambling and tedious.

Rose, who knew a good deal about poetry, was politely silent and clapped with the others at the end of each offering.

Freya contributed a couple of bottles of homemade peapod wine to the party, and drank most of it herself, which in turn led to the astonished women seeing quite another side to the older woman.

"I've lived, you know!" she shrieked, dancing wildly to Frankie's guitar. "I have a past! I was at Greenham Common where I dabbled…" she broke off, but Jo for one had guessed what she was about to say…she'd had a lesbian experience and felt this gave her the cachet of a racy history.

Jo smiled inwardly, wondering not for the first time why straight women felt a tiny bit of sexual tourism, a random, drunken kiss with a woman or even something more gave them a right to align themselves with those who had lived much of their lives in the shadow of society's disapproval and rejection.

Freya had by now pulled out a battered tobacco tin and with difficulty, was rolling a very untidy cigarette. "Hash", thought Frankie instantly. "Oh my god. She's drunk and now she's going to set the barn on fire."

Rose too had twigged to the potential situation, and helped by Elaine, negotiated Freya outside into the courtyard.

"I've always been a free spirit," confided Freya, waving her rollup wildly and dropping ash onto the ground. "I've broken the boundaries, you know," she confided, drunkenly tapping the side of her nose. "I know stuff! And I know stuff about everyone here, too... not everyone is what they seem!" she declared.

Rose and Elaine exchanged glances as they wrapped their coats tighter against the chilly October night. "Maybe we should see you over to your cottage, it's getting late, Freya, and I expect you've things to do before you head off in the morning.

Reluctantly dropping her cigarette, Freya agreed it might be time to get to bed, and allowed the two women to see her indoors and say goodnight.

"She'll have a sore head in the morning," remarked Elaine as they made their way back to the barn. "I hope she forgets most of what she said and did," laughed Rose.

Next day, around noon, Freya was seen emerging from Horseshoes, wearing dark glasses despite the cloudy day, and began piling her belongings into the car. Some of the neighbours came out to say goodbye, but Freya was brusque in her farewells and turned down offers of coffee. "Thank you all, ladies, but I must get down the road before it gets any darker. Ah, my beloved Bearsden! I'm homeward bound again!" She fired the car into life, and with a final wave, disappeared from their lives.

Horseshoes had another temporary inhabitant after Freya: a freelance journalist writing a book on Scotland between the wars was the next tenant, but she kept to herself, taking no part in communal activities, and stayed only a short time.

The next door cottage, Ploughman's Rest, had a few occupants as family and friends of the residents visited for a week or so at a time, but the house seemed reluctant to welcome them. Temporary guests were tolerated, and there was sometimes a faint hesitancy when those staying for a week or so were asked if they liked the cottage: just a beat or two missed before they politely said they'd enjoyed their stay.

More than one visitor mentioned a cold atmosphere in the cottage, so much so that Jennifer had the local plumber call to check that the central heating system was working properly.

"Can't find anything wrong," the plumber told Jennifer. "I've tweaked the thermostat a little, but all the radiators are heating up properly and there's a good supply of hot water. Maybe you need a few draught excluders?"

The stones breathed out, a tiny sigh of relief, as each set of guests left.

Chapter 11
Elaine and Archie

She'd thought she was past all of that side of her life. After everything that had happened, before she managed to get out from under and make a new life for her and Billy – and she had made things as right as she could for her son – she decided that a life focusing on giving them both a good life, and making her businesses thrive, were her priorities.

Men no longer interested her, romantically. They were fine as friends, and she was fond of several long-standing men friends, both married and single, but as partners, they were just too much trouble, too unreliable and generally bad news.

She wasn't going to get caught out again, make herself vulnerable to being hurt, abused, or cheated on by some man.

She had a good life, she told herself. There was money in the bank, she had her lovely home here at Barleyknowe in a safe, friendly community, three thriving hairdressing salons and a good circle of friends. Billy was a successful and happy family man and had given her two beautiful grandchildren. Life was just fine. If there was anything missing, it was a minor irritation, like finishing a jigsaw puzzle to find a couple of pieces are missing. Not the end of the world, really!

That was until she met Archie and suddenly, the closed box of her emotions and deeply buried feelings seemed to be creaking open again, despite her efforts to keep the lid shut.

It was a chance encounter in a hotel in Forfar that brought them together. Elaine had visited the little market town to do some errands and visit an art exhibition in the local gallery and suddenly felt in need of a coffee.

Walking around the town, she found herself outside the hotel where the women had first met up with Jennifer to hear details of life at Barleyknowe.

"This'll do, that wind's biting!" she thought, hurrying into the warmth of the lounge bar and ordering a coffee. Taking off her coat and scarf, she was aware of a faint sound of music and looking round, saw a man playing the piano at the end of the room.

He stopped playing as he caught sight of her, and came over to her table.

"Excuse me, but aren't you one of the ladies who lives out at Barleyknowe? I was playing here the night you all met up and couldn't help but overhear some of your conversation."

Elaine looked at the man, who had very twinkly brown eyes and a broad, open smile below a thick head of dark hair, tinged with grey. There was something cheerful and friendly about him, non-threatening was the word which popped into her head.

She smiled at him, guardedly. "Yes, I'm Elaine Turner and I've bought one of the cottages there. Please join me, I'd love to know more about the area and the history of the farm, if you're local?"

Soon, they were chatting over a pot of coffee, as Archie filled Elaine in on the local area and the farm itself.

"I was born and brought up near here and used to work at Barleyknowe as a schoolboy," said Archie. "We had the tattie holidays in October when us bairns used to make some pocket money hauling up potatoes for a week. Back breaking work, it was, but we loved the few pounds we made!"

Helping himself to a biscuit, he continued: "We all thought it was a shame when the old chap who'd run Barleyknowe for so long had to go into the home, but he just lost heart after his wife died and there were no sons to take over the farm. It was the best thing for him to do, sell up and move into the retirement place."

He smiled. "Somehow, I couldn't see those daughters of his getting their hands dirty mucking out the barn!"

Elaine laughed. "Well, we use the barns for storage of bigger gardening equipment, snow shovels and such like and that's where we'll be storing the crops we produce. Jennifer – she owns the farmhouse and a couple of cottages, as well as the field – has bought a couple of chest freezers for the fruit and veg and has set up hanging poles to dry onions and such like. She's very organised, and seems to have thought of everything!"

She stirred her coffee and went on: "We set up a trestle table to have the occasional communal meal in the barn, but there's no real dirty work for us to do now. I must say, I really like the cottage I bought. It has a history about it, nice thick walls, and a big, solid front door to keep out the weather, but it's been modernised inside. There's a new log burner, a beautiful kitchen and bathroom and central heating and a feeling of cosiness and comfort about the place."

She stopped. "Here's me rattling on! Tell me about yourself, how did you come to work here?"

The time flew by as the pair chatted, and their conversation only ended when the barman discreetly motioned to Archie that he should return to his abandoned piano, as the lounge was filling up with customers.

Archie excused himself, saying "Maybe you'd like to have a drink with me one time?"

They exchanged phone numbers, and Elaine was surprised to notice that she was smiling as she walked back to the car park and headed home through the snow flurries to the sanctuary of her cottage.

Archie carefully added Elaine's number to his mobile phone contacts under the name Elaine Music Shop and smiling, resumed playing a selection of show tunes with renewed enthusiasm.

They always met away from Forfar. Dundee usually, sometimes they went to Arbroath, or further afield to Aberdeen or Perth.

"I like to get away somewhere different when I can," Archie told her as they sat in a Dundee restaurant one evening. "I'm stuck in that hotel lounge churning out the old favourites the clientele seems to love so much. Some nights I'm tempted to stop playing the elevator music and burst into something by Queen or Led Zepplin and watch the faces fall!"

Elaine laughed. Archie was such easy company, he always made her smile. It seemed a very long time since anything or anyone, other than her grandchildren, had made her feel this lightness of spirit, the joyful flutter in her heart. She'd felt able to open up to him about the past in a new way.

"I've told you stuff hardly anyone else knows," she told him one evening. "I don't know why, either, but somehow, you're so easy to talk to, it just seems natural.

There was still a slight, self-protective wariness holding her back, though. Archie was open about his career, music, his upbringing and early, forced marriage to Jean. He talked freely about his sons and grandchildren, his friends, his successes and failures, but she could see a veil dropping when she asked about his wife "See, it's like this, Elaine," Archie began as they sat in the corner of the restaurant sipping coffee at the end of the meal.

Elaine noted that Archie drank only mineral water when they were out, and always did the driving, dropping her discreetly at Barleyknowe road end and staying parked until she texted him to say she was safely indoors.

Both of these courtesies were plus points. "I shouldn't keep thinking that every man is like Michael," she reproached herself. "There are some nice blokes around, I know because I've dated a few, but just never let it develop any further. Maybe I need to take a leap of faith here…"

Drawn from her train of thought, she focused on Archie again and listened to what he was saying.

"I'll not lie to you, Elaine. I still live with Jean, I'm fond of her, she's the mother of my children and she hasn't had it easy living with me. I did the right thing marrying her, it was my child she was carrying, but neither of us really had a choice in the matter. Things might have been different in the cities then, but in a small, rural town, conservative with both a small and large C, and dare I say it? Old fashioned, the opposite of liberal and progressive. I was born and bred in this area, I love the rolling hills, the fresh, clean air and the steady supportiveness of the communities, but… there was a dour and unforgiving attitude to babies born out of wedlock, and towards unmarried mothers, in those times. Girls who were 'caught out' often had to give their babies up for adoption, and there were even cases where the girls' mothers pretended they'd given birth to the baby, so the child grew up thinking his mother was his sister."

He broke off and drank his coffee. "I didn't want that to happen to Jean. I got her pregnant and even though we were both very young, we tried to make a go of things and be good parents."

He looked down at the coffee table, and his voice faltered a little. "I've cheated on Jean over the years. It's not something I'm proud of, I don't want to hurt her, and I've always tried to be discreet. She has discovered my dalliances now and then…" he paused, thinking of the singer at the hotel who was his last fling, their unfortunate chance encounter with a neighbour who saw them together and who then couldn't wait to tell Jean.

"You'll think I'm just saying this, Elaine, but I really care a lot about you. Really a lot. You've become very important to me, you're a very special, very classy lady, who's had a hard time in the past. I want to be honest with you, because I feel something for you I haven't done for a long time."

Elaine looked at him, studying his face. Despite what he'd just said about his cheating on his wife, because that's exactly what it was, however he dressed it up, there was a ring of sincerity about his words.

"He's just trying to get you into bed," said the inner voice of sense which usually predominated in her head. "Ah, but I really like him too," piped up the other voice, the hidden thoughts which she normally suppressed so diligently.

She held his gaze.

"Archie, I've come to really like you, a great deal. Over these last few weeks, you've become very important in my life and that's really something, letting you in after… well, just let's say, I don't take down my barriers easily. I believe you, that you're staying with Jean out of a sense of duty, and suspect, from what you say, you feel more like her brother, or her friend, than her husband."

She saw a startled look flit across his face.

"How, how did you know that?" he exclaimed. "I never said that, but it's true!"

Elaine smiled. "I've worked in hairdressing salons for decades, Archie. Trust me, all life is there. Nothing you could say would surprise me, though it might shock you to learn that many of my ladies say exactly the same about their husbands as you're saying about Jean.

"They tell me: 'He's more like a friend these days, it's companionship we want, somebody to go on holiday with, someone to cook for and someone to do the garden and get the car fixed. And of course, we've the bairns and the grandkids in common…'"

Archie threw back his head and laughed out loud. "I never thought of it the other way round, in all this time. Just shows how self-centred I am, and I guess a lot of men my age think the same. We have big egos and think we're doing the wife a huge favour by staying put!"

"You're in love with him."

The thought came unbidden into Elaine's head.

"No, no. This can't be...in love with a married man, who's still living with his wife. I've always been so careful to protect myself, to stay safe, to keep the rolls of bubble wrap around me, and here I am like a blessed teenager!"

She composed her face, but not before Archie caught her fleeting expression, that softness and openness someone in love can't hide, however much they try to mask their feelings, however carefully they shield their expression.

"My god, she feels the same!" he realised.

He leaned over and took her hand.

A frisson of desire shot through Elaine, causing an involuntary and unbidden clutch in her stomach. This was the first time in the few weeks they'd being seeing each other that there'd been any physical contact, not even a peck on the cheek. She'd liked that too, it showed respect and restraint. But now, at this table, in this corner of the room, with coffee cooling beside their crumpled napkins, the connection fizzled and crackled between them.

A voice, which was hers, but didn't feel like hers, emerged from her throat.

"Come back with me tonight, Archie. Let's give ourselves at least a chance to find some happiness."

Speechless, Archie rose from the table, paid the bill and helped Elaine on with her coat. Breathing in her perfume, his urge to kiss the back of her exposed neck was overwhelming, but he stopped himself, and they left the restaurant arm-in-arm.

There followed weeks of intense passion, love and happiness for the pair. Elaine made it clear after their first night together that she was prepared to be with him, to tolerate his married situation meantime, for the reasons he gave, but if she found out he was seeing anyone else, that would be the end.

"You're not just a fling, Elaine," he assured her. "I really care about you."

They had established a pattern, discreet and sensitive to Archie's situation and to the possible prying eyes at Barleyknowe. "I don't want everyone knowing my business, especially under the circumstances," she told Archie, and he agreed it was best to be careful. Archie would stay over at Elaine's cottage now and then, giving Jean some excuse about playing at a music gig too far away to get back home afterwards on the same night. He'd drop Elaine at the Barleyknowe road end, park in a nearby layby, tucked out of sight, then walk to Springburn, quietly letting himself in by the back door, and always leaving early in the morning before anyone else was awake. Once or twice, they hired a taxi to drop them at the farm road end, and walked the final few hundred yards together. On rare occasions, they stayed together in a hotel, and had the luxury of waking and sharing breakfast together.

"How is this going to work out, Archie?" Elaine asked him after the affair had been going for a few months.

"I just don't know, love," he replied. "We're fine for just now, aren't we?"

She smiled at him, locking eyes, and seeing such love there she felt her heart beat faster in her chest. This is what they mean by happiness, she thought, taking his hand in hers and pulling him towards her for a kiss.

Chapter 12
Sam Taylor Arrives

February 2011

In her Glasgow flat, Angela drew the curtains and closed the door of her study firmly, before taking out a small folder from behind several books on social work methodology and practice. This was a secure hiding place, as Sam never looked at these tomes. This was a far safer hidey-hole than having a second mobile phone or a password-protected folder on her laptop. Sometimes, old methods worked best, she thought, grimly looking at the contents of the folder. She took out a pile of photographs, some slightly out of focus but most clearly showing Sam with an unknown blonde woman, holding hands and kissing. It had been a terrible, dreadful step to ask friends to follow Sam and get the evidence, but she had to know one way or the other if her suspicions had any foundation.

Angela turned the folder over in her hands, trying to ignore the pain she felt at Sam's betrayal. "How could she do this, yet again, after all we've been to each other?" she said, under her breath. She broke off, realising that her fists were clenched so hard that her knuckles were bone white. She hated confrontation, but she wasn't going to be made a fool of again. She'll have it out with Sam that night, see what she said and then decide what she was going to do next.

Sam Taylor walked up the worn stone stairs to the flat, the old dark green tiles lining the walls shining faintly in the dim bulkhead lights of the stairwell. As she climbed to the second floor, she wondered how much longer she could get away with it. She sensed that Angela was suspicious of her many excuses to be out in the evenings and things could get tricky if she started checking up on her flimsy alibis. There was only so much you could ask friends to do for you regarding cover-ups. Was Carol, this latest woman actually worth it, anyway? Yes, she was fine in the sack, as far as that went, and the affair was exciting but that was largely because it had the added thrill of secrecy, but once out of the bedroom she was an utterly boring woman with no conversation and no real interests. She was also becoming too demanding and intense, asking when Sam was going to tell Angela about them, when they were going to be open about their relationship?

Relationship? It was a roll in the hay now and then after drinking, maybe the odd meal out or a trip to a dark, discreet cinema. That wasn't a relationship, with love and commitment, Sam thought cynically. There hasn't been a real, true relationship since Ali and maybe there never would be again...

She opened the flat door with her key and was instantly struck by an unnatural stillness in the atmosphere, although the light was on in the sitting room, so Angela must be home. Sam called out, dropping her keys in the teak bowl on the hall table, and hanging up her jacket.

She took in Angela's still figure, sitting upright and tense on the sofa, and in the same instant she saw the photographs fanned out on the coffee table, the evidence indisputable.

Two hours later, after bitter words, shouting and screaming, tears and recriminations, half-baked apologies from Sam and a torrent of invective from Angela, Sam found herself and her bags on the rainy Glasgow street.

Hailing a taxi, as she couldn't risk driving after the amount of wine she'd had earlier that night with Carol, she was soon in the shelter and anonymity of a Premier Inn. Thank god she had money, Sam mused, not for the first time. She had resources and choices, and could go where she liked, and wasn't tied to a job to earn a living.

Drinking a double gin and tonic from the room's mini bar, Sam sat on the bed and considered her options. "My own flat's got tenants for another year, so I need a place to stay for at least 12 months," she considered. "Where do I want to go?" Opening her phone, she flicked idly through holiday websites, rental properties and offers of writing and art retreats.

'Cottage to let in rural Angus, on 12-18 months basis. Suit artist, writer or someone who seeks a peaceful retreat. The prospective tenant must be female and prepared for life in a small community of women." That's intriguing, thought Sam, most unusual!

She noted down the details on a pad of hotel notepaper, and headed for the shower. It had been a long day, very stressful and traumatic. That bloody Angela, booting her out like that for a bit of extra-curricular nonsense, she grumbled, soaping herself as the hot water ran over her body.

"And how did you feel when Ali did that to you?" That small, inner voice Sam tried always to suppress, spoke up, unbidden.

"Like shit! Kicked in the teeth, she so over-reacted, she knew that I loved her deep down, as much as I can ever love anyone..." Sam quickly switched off the shower and wrapped herself in a huge fluffy bath towel.

"That's never happening again. Never. My heart is bubble wrapped, and I'll do what I want, with who I want, and take what I want, whenever I want from now on. The only feelings I care about are mine, and nobody is getting to me the way Ali did, not ever again!"

Sam realised she was talking out loud, and switched on the TV for company.

As the Antiques Roadshow signature tune began, the newly-uncoupled woman tried to distract herself by concentrating on the stream of treasures being brought by the public to the experts, all in the hopes of surprise windfalls from their old vases and collections of postcards.

"Sad bastards," thought Sam, pouring another gin. On screen, an elderly woman proffered a small china figurine for inspection. Watching the woman chat, Sam was suddenly reminded of her late mother.

"Let's not go there," she said, again out loud, and changed the channel. Tomorrow was another day, and she's look into the Angus cottage situation. Maybe a change of scene was just what she needed? She'd be best being far away from Angela and that dopey blonde woman Carol. Fresh fields were what she needed, and where fresher than the Angus countryside?

"This could be the chance to pick up my painting again," Sam mused. "A company of women, too! Now that could be interesting."

***

Sam's arrival at Barleyknowe two weeks later was observed by all of the other residents. There had been a heavy snow fall the day before and the farm road and courtyard were piled high with drifts. The electricity was cutting out off and on, as was the internet, so the women had to focus on what they could reasonably do in the meantime.

"We need to get this lot cleared," Jo said to Maureen as they shared a pot of coffee at Marchmont the following morning, which happened to be a Saturday.

"Indeed we do," Maureen agreed. "I've a snow shovel and a spade in the hut and will fetch them out as soon as we've finished our coffee."

Jo smiled at her. "It's no surprise to me how organised you are, Maureen! I'll bet your ward was always in perfect order, just like this place!" Her gaze travelled round the room, where they sat in two comfortable armchairs in front of the log burner. Everything was clean, tidy and organised, from the shelves of books to the fireside basket with its neatly stacked pile of logs and kindling.

"Well, I like order in my life," Maureen admitted, pouring out more coffee and offering a plate of shortbread. "It's good to be able to find things easily. My mother used to say you should put things back in their place as soon as you've used them. That way, no clutter and confusion!"

Jo smiled, and thought of her own house next door. She kept Dairy Cottage clean, of course, but it was definitely messier than Maureen's place. Maybe she should take a leaf out of the former nurse's book and be a bit more organised?

She watched Maureen sipping the hot drink and it suddenly struck her, for the first time, what an attractive woman she was, as well as being a nice person. The years had been kind to her, and although her hair was grey, it was well cut and her skin was virtually unlined. Jo observed her more closely, if surreptitiously, and saw a trim figure and long, slender hands. As she rose to clear the table, her long, shapely legs were apparent even under the jeans she wore.

Maureen turned and smiled broadly at her neighbour. "I'll go and fetch the shovels and we'll get started, ok?"

"Yes, of course." Jo rose and reached for her jacket and gloves, all the while wondering what on earth had just happened." Could it be...no, stop being so ridiculous, you're just starting to let your imagination run riot!" she told herself firmly.

"This is a straight, older woman with no thoughts of you except as a neighbour. You are a stupid, silly old woman, Jo!"

Grasping the offered shovel, she opened the cottage door, striding out to begin the task of clearing an area. As Maureen closed the door behind her and stepped onto the path, she slid on some frozen earth. Jo caught her before she fell completely forward and steadied her upright.

"The last thing we want are any broken bones, lady!" she joked.

Maureen smiled. "No, I don't fancy a trip to hospital in this weather, nor having to wear a cast for weeks: thank you!"

Maureen felt her heart beating a little too fast. "Must have been the shock of almost falling there," she thought, picking up the spade. "No, it wasn't" said that inner voice which always told her the truth, whether she wanted to hear it or not. "It was Jo's arms around you for a few seconds that set your heart racing! When are you going to face up to this one?"

"Oh stop it!" She spoke out loud, causing Jo to turn round, astonished.

"Sorry," said Maureen, her face flushing. "I was just wishing it would stop snowing so we could clear a path!"

Jo smiled, and they were working in harmonious silence when gradually, other cottage doors opened and women emerged, carrying spades and shovels. They'd cleared the courtyard and were starting to work on the farm track, when the sound of a car labouring up the road made them stop and listen.

A 4x4 was navigating the treacherous roadway, coming to a careful halt outside Horseshoes. The engine was stilled, and a figure emerged from the driving seat. Flinging back the hood of her parka to reveal a pixie-shaped face topped with beautifully cut blonde hair, the woman stepped down to the ground, smiling.

"Hi, I'm Sam Taylor, and you must be my neighbours. I'll just get the keys from the farmhouse, then you must come indoors and tell me everything about life here. Then I'll help with the snow clearing!"

The assembled women returned her greetings and then watched in silence as she walked towards the farmhouse, tramping across the partly-cleared courtyard in a pair of very expensive-looking red boots

"Well, that lady knows how to dress," said Elaine, the first to speak. Frankie gazed at the retreating figure. "Jeezo! What a beautiful woman, those legs are endless!"

Irene and Rose also watched Sam as she knocked at Jennifer's door. There was an odd stillness about Irene, as if she was holding her breath, Rose noticed.

The moment was broken as Jennifer opened the door and smiling, handed the keys of Horseshoes to the new tenant.

"I'll be out to join you in just a moment," she called. "I had some urgent work to finish now the internet is back up and running, honestly, I'm not ducking out of snow clearing! Maybe you'd all like a hot drink here before we carry on with our efforts: yes, you too, Sam, come in here before you unpack! And turn up the heating in Horseshoes, it's only on low just now!"

The women put down their spades and, leaving their boots in the farmhouse porch, went indoors to have a warming drink and get to know their new, temporary neighbour.

Chapter 13
Trouble Looms

"Sam's quite out of my league! She's too young, too pretty, too sophisticated and definitely out of the question, entirely!" Irene told herself sharply, on one of the many nights she couldn't sleep and had gone downstairs so as not to wake Rose. "You're an idiot to think she would even consider you, and even if she did, I know the type! A player if ever I saw one…and what of Rose? She doesn't deserve me even having these thoughts!"

Irene had been aware, the moment Sam stepped down from her car that snowy day, how attractive she was, how charismatic and appealing, but had stifled the thoughts. That very morning, on social media, she'd seen a silly cartoon of a brain pointing to a heart and captioned: "I'm with stupid here!" How very, sadly true, Irene mused.

The first real encounter she'd had with the new resident was a week or so after Sam's arrival.

Rose had driven to Arbroath for some much-needed supplies now that the roads were less treacherous, leaving Irene at home to catch up with some chores around the cottage. Irene was hoovering when she heard a brisk knock at the door. She opened it to find Sam, muffled against the keen wind, and with an apologetic smile brightening her face.

"My god, this woman is stunning!" was Irene's instant thought, but she quickly composed her expression and asked Sam indoors out of the cold.

"I'm so sorry to disturb you," Sam said, taking off her wet boots in the porch. "I can't seem to override the central heating controls and can't lay my hands on the instruction manual. I've tried Jennifer's door but there's no answer and wondered if you could help? I think we all have the same boiler system!" Sam stood upright, placing her boots neatly on the newspaper laid out for just this purpose, then she ran her hand through her hair, brushing off the droplets.

At this gesture, Irene felt a wave of desire shudder through her, unbidden, unwanted, dangerous, powerful and overwhelming. The urge to fold Sam in her arms and kiss her was almost unbearable. To hide her feelings, she coughed and turned away a little, but not before Sam had caught and understood Irene's expression. So many people had fallen for her over so many years, she was perfectly attuned to the effect she had on both women and men and knew instantly what Irene was thinking and feeling.

"That didn't take long! I must still have it..." she thought. Then, "Well, who knows? This is an older woman, not unattractive. We'll see what happens."

Nothing did happen that day except Irene was able to quickly reset the boiler at Horseshoes for Sam and also located the instruction booklets for her. They'd been left, presumably by the last tenant, at the very back of the hall cupboard under a pile of bin bags.

"Thanks so much," said Sam. "I thought I'd looked everywhere but I must have missed them. Would you like a coffee before you go home?"

Irene, who'd by now managed to compose herself and deal with the practicalities, turned down the offer of a coffee pleading a list of chores to get through before Rose returned.

"Well, maybe next time," said Sam, smiling again. "I'd like to get to know everyone, after all, I'm going to be here for a while!"

It took more contact, more meetings, in the company of others and then alone, before anything did happen.

"I'm on a bloody cliff edge here," Irene, tormented, thought one morning as she stacked logs in a basket from their woodshed, and refilled the bird feeders. Rose was indoors, ironing, interspersed with blowing her nose, which was red raw.

"I'll go outside this time," she told Rose. "That cough of yours sounds sore. You need to stay warm.

"Oh, it's just a cold, I'll soon be fine," Rose replied, after a burst of coughing. "I might miss the do at Sam's tonight, though, I don't want to spread the germs. A night by the fire here in my dressing gown with a hot toddy is what I want!"

Irene smiled and pulled on a jacket and boots to go out into the cold.

"I should just avoid Sam entirely, stay well away from her, but, I just can't. I want to see her, be in her company, even though this is just crazy stuff. She won't look twice at me," she muttered, savagely hauling kindling and logs into the basket. "I'm an idiot, a fool, just a fool!"

That evening, as Rose sat by the fire nursing her cold, Irene packed a basket with wine and some snacks and headed across the courtyard to Sam's. The door opened almost instantly to her knock, and Sam ushered her in.

"Just hang your coat there, yes, just above the radiator and it'll keep it dry. Come into the fire, now is it red or white for you…oh thanks, you didn't need to bring anything, it's all here! I'm afraid it's only you, me, Maureen and Jo tonight. Jennifer's in London, Frankie's in Edinburgh for a couple of weeks and I think Elaine's off to visit her son down south."

Irene sat on one of the pair of couches by the fire, across from Maureen and Jo, who were already sipping wine and chatting.

Something about their body language made Irene look at them more closely, under cover of accepting the glass of wine Sam put in her hand.

"Animated!" That was the word, Irene thought, looking at the pair across from her. Although Maureen's voice was croaky, she was cheerful and chatty. "She's taken down a few barriers recently," mused Irene, "so different from the stand-offish woman she was when she first came here. Jo seems lighter too, less burdened, somehow. I wonder, no, surely not, Maureen's straight and if you ask me, at heart, quite inhibited, no, could it be? A late-life romance on the other side of the fence? Jo looks different, happier, I'm not quite sure…"

Her train of thought was broken as Jo enquired after Rose's health.

"Oh, it's just a cold, I'm hoping it doesn't settle in her chest though, she's asthmatic and that's always a worry. She's staying put meantime!"

"Can't take any chances," said Maureen. "If she's no better in a few days, make sure she sees the doctor. I'd offer to visit but my throat is starting to feel scratchy and I don't want to give her anything else."

After a couple of hours chatting about Barleyknowe, what brought them there and of course, the weather, Maureen put down her glass and said, ruefully: "I'm sorry, Sam, but my throat really is bothering me. I'm sure it's a wretched cold coming on and there's nothing for it but to get to my bed with a hot lemon drink. It's been a lovely evening and I'm sad to be cutting it short, but…"

Sam stood up. "Not a problem, Maureen, I just hope you feel better soon. Have you plenty of food in case you're stuck in for a few days? I can let you have milk and eggs..." She turned towards the kitchen and her 'fridge, when Jo too got to her feet. Her haste was obvious to Irene, who was still sitting at the fireside.

"I've a dozen eggs bought today and a couple of pints of extra long-life milk, Maureen. Why don't we pop in at mine now and that's you set up for a few days indoors?"

Maureen smiled, and croaked a 'thank you', allowing Sam to fetch her coat and scarf.

"Almost like a teenage boy on his first date," thought Irene, watching Jo hold open the door for Maureen. "Jo's an experienced, older woman but she's behaving with the gaucheness of a sixteen-year-old! She's got it bad."

The door closed behind the women and Sam came back into the sitting room, rubbing her hands together.

"Wow, it's cold out there tonight!" She leaned past where Irene was sitting, about to lift a couple of applewood logs from the fireside basket. Irene sat perfectly still, frozen into immobility, as the sleeve of Sam's silk shirt brushed her arm. Without thinking, without any hesitation, Irene caught the younger woman's arm, holding it lightly. Sam stopped in mid-movement and slowly, carefully, leant down and cupped Irene's face with her hands, kissing her with great tenderness.

Irene gasped, a low moan, and then she pulled Sam to her on the couch, kissing her with a fierce, pent-up longing and passion. They were locked, kissing, for several minutes, until Sam made an exploratory gesture, touching Irene's breasts through her shirt, and beginning to undo the buttons.

"No, stop! I mustn't!" Irene, flushed, her breath labouring, sprang to her feet. "I, I'm so sorry, Sam, you're wonderful and attractive and I want you with every fibre of my being, I have since you first arrived here, but…" she tailed off, her voice ragged.

Cool, in charge of the situation, Sam took her hand. "It's ok, Irene. I know, I get it. You're with Rose, and you love her. It's fine. But maybe you should go home now before anything else happens."

Irene wiped away the tears which had begun to fall, and hurried to grab her coat and boots, opening the door. "I'm, I'm so sorry, Sam…thank you…"

A minute later she was quietly opening her own front door, and peeping in the bedroom, was relieved to find that Rose was sound asleep and snoring.

Irene tiptoed into the bathroom and then headed for the spare bedroom. Thank god she had the perfect excuse to sleep apart from Rose until the cold had gone. She needed time to think, to sort out her jumbled thoughts and deal with the guilt that she felt.

Across at Horseshoes, Sam poured herself a whisky and sat by the dying fire for a while. A smirk flitted across her beautiful face as she replayed the events of half an hour earlier.

"If I want you, Irene Fraser, I will have you. And now it's game on, and I do want you." Knocking back the dregs of the whisky, she carried plates and glasses through to the kitchen, locked up, damped down the fire and went to bed. Tomorrow was another day…

The first the women knew of Rose's deterioration was the arrival of an ambulance outside Glen View the next morning, and paramedics helping Rose into the back of the vehicle. A distraught-looking Irene ran to the carpark and soon the ambulance, followed by Irene in her car, set off down the farm track, heading for Dundee.

Later that day, Irene was seen parking her car behind the barn, and both Jo and Sam came out to speak to her.

"Rose took a really bad asthma attack in the early hours of the morning," said Irene, "and it just isn't worth chancing things. She's been hospitalised a few times in the past with her asthma, so NHS 24 suggested an ambulance to take her to hospital. She's much better this afternoon, but they want to keep her in hospital for a couple of days till they're sure she's well enough to come home."

Irene spoke to Jo, avoiding Sam's gaze, but the young woman spoke, calmly.

"She's in the best place, Irene. There's more snow forecast for tonight and it might have been much more difficult to get her to hospital by tomorrow."

"I'm going in to visit her tomorrow," Irene replied, ignoring Sam's comment about the weather. "We'll see how she is then."

"Do give Rose our love," Jo said, giving Irene an unexpected hug. "Please let me know if there's anything I can do to help, and look after yourself! You look done in!"

"Thanks," said Irene, "now, I'm going in for a nap!"

***

The weather forecast which Sam had seen online earlier that day was accurate, and a major snowstorm hit the area overnight, blanketing Tayside in a fresh, deep coating of snow, plummeting the temperatures and closing the smaller roads. Schools were closed and there were a number of power outages as the weight of snow collapsed the lines. A fierce, chilling wind which blew the top layers of snow onto newly cleared roads and pavements added to the difficulties in getting around. Radio Tay and the local councils advised people to stay at home if possible and to check on their elderly or vulnerable neighbours.

Irene looked out at the blizzards sweeping down from the glens next morning, as she drank a cup of tea, and realised immediately, even before listening to the forecast, that she'd be stuck here, as would all the other residents of Barleyknowe. Elaine was still in Manchester, Frankie staying put in Edinburgh meantime and Jennifer was working in London for a further week anyway, they'd all discovered from the Barleyknowe Facebook group they'd kept active even after they'd all moved in to the cottages

She phoned the hospital later that morning to have her predictions confirmed. Rose was more settled, but was being kept in for observation and wouldn't be allowed home meantime for medical reasons. The staff nurse explained that they did have a system for returning patients home in bad weather, using 4x4 vehicles, but there were still concerns about Rose's condition, so she'd be staying put meantime.

There was nothing to be done but to sit this out.

That evening, Irene sitting watching TV when she was surprised to hear a knock at her door. The curtains were drawn against the bleak night, but she resisted the temptation to peep out and see her caller.

Framed in the doorway was Sam. Her hands were stuffed into the pockets of her coat, but her head was bare and already, snowflakes were glistening on her hair. She said nothing, but followed Irene silently through into the sitting room and slowly removed her coat, hanging it over a chair.

"How's Rose?" asked Sam, her voice quiet.

"A little bit better, but she'll be in hospital for a few days yet. They can't get her home anyway, with this weather," Irene said flatly. "Would you like a drink?" she added, suddenly unsure as to what to say or do.

Sam didn't reply, but instead, moved towards Irene and took her in her arms. She felt the woman freeze, then relax into her embrace. They kissed long and hard, until Sam broke away.

"This is just us, just for you and me, Irene. We want each other, we both know that. Rose will never know, she'll never find out if we're discreet, and we will be very careful to make sure that she never knows and is never hurt. This is us, our time, and it's separate and apart from your relationship with her. It'll be exciting and fun! I know you're bored, I can tell. This, us, you and me, might bring back some fire into your relationship. I don't want to break you and Rose up, I just don't want this chance for us to go by. You're a very attractive, sexy woman, Irene, but I don't suppose you need me to tell you that…"

She paused, waiting for Irene to speak.

Wordlessly, Irene took her hand and led her upstairs to the spare bedroom.

The atmosphere at Barleyknowe was changing. The stones of the houses tightened imperceptibly and moaned silently, as a subtle but growing feeling of unease and tension permeated the community.

Home a couple of weeks later in the farmhouse, Jennifer suffered cruelly as she went through the pain of unrequited love for Frankie, compounded by what she called 'the Sam factor'. Until Sam arrived at Horseshoes, Jennifer had gradually been getting closer to Frankie over the months, sharing the occasional trip to a local art exhibition or music event, and chatting over a coffee or a glass of wine. There was undoubtedly a spark there between them, but both women were wary of involvement and hurt, as they'd discussed candidly, and by unspoken agreement, they let the obvious connection between them develop at a slow and steady pace.

Neither had made a sexualised move towards the other as yet, confining their contact to a hug and peck on the cheek, but were both aware of the direction of travel, as Jennifer thought of it. "No rush," Jennifer told herself. "We're getting to know each other, learn our histories, open up to each other, and become the best of friends first."

Frankie too had been attracted to the older woman.
"You've got mummy issues," Johnny had once told her as Frankie got ready for a date with a woman twenty years her senior.

"You're havering, Johnny, I'm not listening to your half-baked pop psychology," she'd retorted, spraying herself liberally with Opium.

"I like older women because they're mature, experienced and usually past all the dramas and angsting that goes on with young women. They tend to be more interesting, too, because they've seen a done things, had a life!

"Yeah, but what about all the wrinkles and saggy bits?" he'd retorted.

Frankie threw a cushion at him and pulled on her jacket. "You're so superficial, Johnny! Looks aren't everything, bodies are there to be celebrated at every stage of life. Just think yourself lucky that I'll always love you, even when you're a decrepit old geezer!" Suitably chastened, Johnny chuckled. "Ok, ok, have a good time with Mrs Methuselah!" and ducked as Frankie hurled another cushion at his head.

Cooking fish for herself and Misty one evening, Frankie thought about Jennifer and where this friendship was heading. She found herself thinking a lot about the older woman, and looking forward eagerly to their occasional jaunts.

"Hmmm. I just don't know," she told Misty, who was sitting in anticipation at her mistress's feet. "I like Jennifer a lot, really a lot, we have fun together, there's a good, easy friendship there, and there's a spark of attraction, I admit that, but do I want it to go further? Am I over Marion, enough to take a chance? And what if it all goes wrong, I'll have lost a good friend and it could be awkward living a few doors away from her! What do you think, Misty?"

As is the way of cats, Misty said nothing, but looked inscrutable.

"You're no help!" said Frankie, taking some fish from the pan to cool in Misty's feeding bowl. "I guess I'll just need to sort this one out myself, pussy cat. Maybe I need more time?"

Her inner voice nudged her. "This isn't about Jennifer, and you bloody well know it, lady. You like Jen, of course you do, you like her very much indeed, and you fancy her, she's a very attractive woman and she's the safer option, but you know what you feel for Sam, that gut wrenching attraction and desire, the huge tug and pull. You're in denial because you can't cope with this intensity of feeling all over again, with the thought of being pulled to the clifftop and crashed to the rocks…"

"Oh, shut the fuck up!" Frankie shouted out loud, drowning her inner voice and causing Misty to look up from her bowl. "I can't even contemplate going through this stuff again with someone like Sam, who'll break my heart and bugger off back to Glasgow without a thought. That's if she's even noticed me like that! Probably she hasn't, she's much too sexy and glamorous for somebody like me, and I'd be punching well above my weight with that lady! Jennifer really cares about me, I don't think she'll mess me around, it would be nice to have somebody to love again… maybe I should give it a whirl with Jen and take my mind off this silly infatuation with Sam…I don't even think she's that nice a person, there's something about her I just can't put my finger on, who does she remind me of, Misty?"

She washed and dried the dishes, then suddenly dropped the tea towel.

"Of course! Sam reminds me of that bloody woman from Glasgow I dated for all of six weeks, or was it seven?"

Misty gave no reply, so Frankie mulled over the memory.

"Bella! That was her name! It's all coming back to me now. That's who Sam reminds me of, Bella! A beautiful woman, fabulous clothes, a sparkling wit, great fun and we had a good time, but she turned out to be a total control freak, selfish and a player with a capital P. She flirted with other women, and I suspect was unfaithful to me, even in the short time we were together. I remember now how uncomfortable she made me feel when we were in company, all those little digs and innuendoes and sexual hints, and she was so indiscreet. Right, I need to be really careful around her, and keep my guard up. And I need to shift my thinking around about Jennifer: this could really work, I should give it a whirl!"

A few yards away, in the farmhouse, Jennifer was closing up her work computer for the day and tidying her desk. It was an extravagance, but she kept a computer and smart phone purely for business and an iPad for personal emails, documents and social media, just as she had done when working in London. That way, even though her study was part of her home, she could separate her working and private lives.

She switched on the iPad and began checking her personal emails, all the while glancing out of the window into the winter evening.

Lights were on in all the cottages except the empty Ploughman's Rest, no guests of the residents being there in the dead of winter. Jennifer watched as the women prepared their meals, stoked fires and settled down for the evening to watch TV, read or chat.

Jennifer's eye was drawn to Meadowfields, and she saw Frankie at the sitting room window, the lamplight behind her, her arms raised as she pulled the curtains closed.

"Come to me, Frankie. Be mine, love me as I love you," she whispered. "Let's begin our story, with hope and love. Walk those few yards to me, fold into my arms, let me kiss you, kiss me back. I won't let you down. I'll treat you with the kindness which you deserve, I'll make you happy again…"

The stones listened and heard the whisper, and knowing, with the wisdom of centuries how things should work out for the best, carried the faint words through the winter air, whisking them into Meadowfields, and landing them in Frankie's restless brain, as she sat at the fireside, unable to concentrate on her book.

Eventually, she threw down the paperback, and went to the window, carefully peeping through the curtains. Jennifer's sitting room lights were on, giving a warm glow through the closed curtains.

Frankie went into the bathroom and stared at herself in the mirror for several minutes. In her head, thoughts began to settle and clarify, focus emerged. There was something driving her forward, something odd and strange yet persuasive, as if a voice was whispering in her ear, yet she could only really hear the faint noise of the wind blowing round the huddled cottages.

She cleaned her teeth thoroughly, renewed her make-up and sprayed on some perfume, before changing her clothes, damping down the fire in the log burner and closing the door. Taking a bottle of red wine from the rack in her kitchen, dousing the candles and lights and zipping up her coat, she left Meadowfields, quietly locking the door.

A minute later, she knocked on the door of the farmhouse, which was quickly opened by Jennifer. For several moments, they stood in silence in the hall, just looking at each other, their eyes locking, serene and still.

"You wanted me to come and I have," said Frankie, putting the bottle of wine on the hall table but not moving her gaze from the other woman.

Jennifer said nothing, but a smile began to form, illuminating her face. Slowly, and with great tenderness, she unzipped Frankie's jacket and hung it on peg.

"Sit down," she said quietly, gently lowering Frankie to a chair below the pegs. With deliberate, unhurried care, she removed Frankie's boots, caressing her feet sensually as she did so. Then she took her hand and led her upstairs to her bedroom.

She was closing the long, thick bedroom curtains when she sensed Frankie behind her, her perfume filling the air, as the younger woman slid her hands under Jennifer's shirt and unbuttoned her bra, cupping her breasts from behind and gently rolling the erect nipples between her thumbs and fingers.

Jennifer turned, her breath already coming in short gasps, and took Frankie's face in her hands, kissing her long and deeply and hearing, with delight, the gasp and moan of pleasure this brought in the woman.

With exquisite sensitivity and knowing there was all the time in the world, the women undressed each other and slid into the coolness of Jennifer's bed. They made love throughout the winter night, giving and receiving pleasure, until their bodies were familiar with the knowledge of love.

As the dawn broke pink over the snowy fields, heralding another day of snow, the lovers finally untangled and Frankie dressed speedily.

"I'll go back to my place," she said to the offers of tea and a shower from Jennifer. "Misty'll be giving me a ticking off if I'm not there for breakfast!"

Jennifer laughed, and kissed her with great tenderness and longing, before opening the heavy front door. "See you later, very soon!" whispered Frankie, giving her a last hug before she slipped out into the courtyard and hurried through the early snowflakes to Meadowfields, where she almost tripped over Misty, who was lying right at the front door.

"Let me in, you daft cat! I've lots to tell you!" Frankie laughed.

Across the courtyard at Horseshoes, Sam Taylor was staring out of her bedroom window. Unable to sleep after a nightmare which woke her in the early hours, she'd made tea and sat at the window for a long time, watching the snow and reflecting on her life, which wasn't pleasing her at the moment.

She was just about to leave the window seat to return to bed, when a movement caught her eye. As she watched, the door of the farmhouse opened slowly and out stepped Frankie. Half-hidden in the doorway was Jennifer, but Sam clearly saw the two women lean into a kiss, a proper kiss, not an innocent embrace between friends.

Stepping quickly back from the window so as not to be seen, Sam watched Frankie hurry to her own cottage and open and close the door.

"Well, well, so that's what's going on!" Sam thought. "That's very interesting, very interesting indeed!"

She stood, lost in thought for a minute, and then spoke out loud to the empty room. "I wonder just how easy it's going to be to take young Frankie away from the boss lady and get her into my bed? That's a challenge, but I think that girl has taken a shine to me anyway, as have several others if I'm not mistaken! This could be a bit of sport for these dreary winter months. I'll just need to manage Irene carefully!"

The stones heard, but their powers were limited in the face of such darkness.

Sam drew her curtains closed against the dawn and went back to her bed, a smile playing about her lips as she pulled the duvet over her elegant body and fell fast asleep.

***

During the days of early spring, Sam spent most mornings painting, drawing on the local scenery for inspiration. If the weather was reasonable, she'd wrap up well and drive to the Angus Glens, or to the seaside towns, where she'd sketch for an hour or so at a time, until it was too cold to sit still any longer.

As she sketched, she pondered.

"What should I do next?" she mused, drawing the first rough outline of a seagull perched on the harbour wall at Arbroath. "Should I go back to Glasgow and try to make amends with Angela? Maybe I've blown that one completely, and actually, do I want to resume a relationship with her? She wasn't a barrel of laughs, and was starting to bore me.

"Maybe I should take back my own place once the tenants leave and start afresh with a new project, some work, a new woman? I don't want any more to do with that dozy Carol, that's for sure. She was getting far too intense for my peace of mind."

Sam reached into her jacket pocket for the fingerless gloves she always carried, pulled them on and continued drawing the bird, which helpfully stood still, only its feather ruffled and tugged by the rising wind.

"You know Irene has strong feelings for you, but you don't love her. She's just a bit of fun, a dalliance, to show yourself you can still do this! When are you going to let the confidence you show to others actually become real, in your heart? You know how people look at you, admire you, want you, why do you have to keep on proving yourself with all these women you pick up and drop without a thought?" Sam's inner dialogue rolled on as she sketched. Not one to share confidences with others, she was always privately brutally honest with herself, but her conscience was a weak, fragile part of her makeup and easily squashed.

"What does it matter?" Sam thought, quickly dismissing her better feelings and vestiges of any sympathy for Irene. "She's the one doing the cheating on that poor, insipid woman, Rose. I'm single and free, and Irene knows I'm not looking for a serious relationship with her, I made that clear at the very start. It's her lookout if things go pear-shaped with Rose, or if she gets hurt when I end it with her, which I definitely will. I'm not responsible for her feelings for me… I'm being careful, and Irene's enjoying the fun, and the sex, when she isn't angsting over how's she's cheating on Rose. That's getting pretty tedious, actually. Maybe I'll just draw it to a close sooner rather than later!"

Many people, over many years, had remarked on the disconnect between Sam's angelic, beautiful, outward appearance and her heart of granite.

"You should come with a fucking health warning, like a packet of fags!" one disillusioned lover had said to her, bitterness in her voice. "You treat people like utter shit, Sam, picking them up as if they were toys for you to play with and tossing them aside, with no regard for their feelings, the minute you get weary of them, or if someone smarter, sexier or more fun comes along. You think you're a great lover because you know how to give pleasure, but what I want, what most women want, is a proper connection, genuine feelings, messiness, passion, even mistakes and nervous clumsiness from a sincere lover, but not this clinical detached way you are, like it's a job of work to make me climax, a project to be completed so you can tick the box! What has made you like this? Or were you just born without any empathy, any moral compass, any genuine desires, or any real feelings?"

Putting on her jacket and picking up the carrier bag of the clothes and toiletries she'd kept at the woman's house for convenience on the nights she stayed over, Sam shrugged, unmoved by the woman's words, or her obvious distress.

"It's all just a game, really! We had a bit of fun, a few laughs, some good times, but now it's over. It's no big deal. You'll soon find someone else," Sam added, heading for the door. "I'm really not worth shedding tears over, nobody is. Take care, you'll soon forget about me!"

With that, she left, but the woman's parting words rang in her ears.

"There's such a thing as Karma, Sam Taylor. This will all backfire on you one day, and I hope I hear about it. Hell mend you, you utter bitch!"

Putting the finishing touches to the sketch of the seagull, Sam remembered the old incident and how she'd carefully avoided answering the rhetorical question flung by the spurned lover, and kept her bland composure.

Walking away that day – how many years ago? five? six maybe? towards her car, the angry ex's tirade still ringing in her ears, she'd known which barbs had struck home .

Now, alone at Arbroath harbour, drawn back to the past, Sam thought again about the incidents which had shaped her life. No, of course she hadn't always been like this, a charismatic, but cold and callous bitch.

As a child, she'd cared deeply for the people around, her parents, her pets, her school friends and of course, Nanny Brown.

"Maybe if I hadn't been sent off at seven to boarding school, losing my darling Nanny who loved me so, so dearly, even if no-one else did, parted from the dog and cats and hardly seeing my parents after that, except in the school holidays, it might have been different," she thought, remembering the pain of separation, the homesickness in the unfamiliar school where she knew no-one and where she was frightened, lonely and sad.

"If my bloody mother hadn't been so caught up with her social life and trips abroad, and my fucking father had cared a tenth as much about me as he did that tart of a mistress, I might have turned out to be a better person!" she thought angrily, unlocking the car and flinging her sketch pad and pencils into the boot. "Hypocrites! Cold-hearted, callous people who didn't deserve to have a daughter, or to treat me as they did. Money doesn't make up for lack of attention and love for a child."

Ali. That was the nearest she'd ever come to letting another person in after that, and look how that had turned out!

"I can't do this anymore, Sam" Ali had wept, that final day together. "I love you, I really do, but I can't put up with this lack of commitment from you any longer. We've been together for three years now, and lived together for two, but I never feel safe with you. I'm convinced you would dump me at the drop of a hat, I know that you see other women and I just can't take it anymore.

"Have you even the slightest idea how I feel, knowing you're off with someone else, afraid she'll take you away from me for good? I'm tired of making excuses when my family asks why you won't come to visit them with me, why my partner is always so busy, why she goes on holiday with other people, why we don't buy a house together or do any of the normal things which couples take in their stride?"

"Don't end it with me, Ali," Sam had pleaded. "I'll change, I'll stop playing around and I'll visit your family if it means so much…" she tailed off, watching Ali's expression harden.

"We've had this conversation so many times, Sam," Ali reminded her. "It's always the same: you promise to change, and you don't. You say that you'll see someone about your issues, you'll do anything to keep me, I relent, and a few weeks later there's no sign of an appointment with a counsellor or therapist, and you're back to the same old ways! Maybe you can't change? I'm not a psychologist, I don't know why you're like this, but I do know that I'm worth more than to be treated like this. I have to end it with you, once and for all, or I'll just go mad."

Weeping, distraught, Ali cried: "Just go now, and collect the rest of your things next week. Pick a day I'm out at work, and put your keys through the letterbox. I'll send on your mail if you leave me an address, but I don't want to see you again, Sam. Not ever. Don't phone me, don't email, don't write to me and above all, don't come to my house again. It's over, and that's the end of it!"

Ali's tears overwhelmed her again, and Sam left, in a daze.

Ali was the one woman she'd been the nearest to really loving someone, to caring for her feelings, but true to form, she'd pressed the self-destruct button yet again and turned her away.

Hell mend me indeed, Sam thought wryly, turning the car round in the car park and heading towards her temporary home.

"Yes, but Ali, but nobody, knows what you went through," she reminded herself, as she manoeuvred the car onto the main road.

The boarding school experience had been truly traumatic for the small child. Still today, as a mature woman, her face flushed hot as she recalled the daily, morning shame of admitting to wet sheets, the incessant bullying from other, older girls who called her names like 'smelly Nelly!' and 'Miss pee the bed!'

At seven, she was a dumpy, plain-looking child, very far removed from the beautiful, willowy blonde she'd later become. She didn't do well academically, although she'd been good at drawing and painting, and the art room becoming her refuge over the years.

"It might have been alright if I'd been welcome at home in the holidays!" Sam mused, as she drove through the bleak Angus countryside. "I was lucky to get an hour a day with mother, and even then she was distracted with her own preoccupations! I just didn't cut it for her, a timid, frightened little rabbit of a kid who wasn't even pretty. And as for dad, when did I ever even see him?"

Escape from school at 18, with enough exam passes to get her into art college, had been the turning point for Sam, who found her niche and made a few friends.

At the time, she observed with some amazement how her physical appearance seemed to alter in response to a happier life, no more comfort eating brought her the figure she's always craved and in turn, her burgeoning but still fragile confidence began to draw people to her. She was liked, and desired, and wanted by men and women alike.

"That wasn't going to last though, was it?" Sam remembered grimly. Her first two lovers at art college, Ben, and then later, Tara, both dumped her quite brutally, finding her hard going and her overwhelming neediness too big a price to pay, despite her fabulous looks and her obvious artistic talent.

Ben had been abrupt with her. "It's no good, Sam, I just can't deal with your jealousies. It doesn't matter how many times I tell you I'm not cheating on you, you need proof, somehow. I feel you'd like to put some sort of tag on me, to check my every move! And, I'm sorry, but I can't give you any guarantees about how long we'll last as a couple. We're young, still at college, I don't know how I'm going to feel about you in a few months, far less forever and a day! I'm sorry, Sam, but I just can't deal with you and this level of intensity."

Tara had been kinder, but said much the same as Ben had done.

"You're just too high maintenance, honey," Tara told her, that last day, as she picked up her few belongings from Sam's flat. "I'm no psychologist, but you really need to sort out this issue about your folks or it's going to dog you all your life. You're a gorgeous woman and lot of fun when you let you hair down, but I'm looking for a girlfriend, for an easy relationship which is fun and laughs, not a person so hung up, suspicious and oh my god, so needy!"

"I really had strong feelings for Tara," thought Sam. "Almost as much as I did for Ali. Maybe because she was my first woman lover, or maybe because she seemed to care so much for me? Who knows, but she kicked me to the kerb just as Ben had done the year before!"

After her rejection by Tara, something hardened in her, she knew that, and no amount of the therapy she'd had, secretly, was enough to change her for the better.

"I vowed after Tara threw me over that nobody would ever hurt me, never get to me again," she remembered, grimly. "Ali nearly did, but I cleared off in time. Nobody has gotten to me since, and no-one is getting to me ever again!"

Driving carefully through the melting slush, she remembered how she'd felt that night in the hotel after Angela kicked her out. She's vowed just to do as she pleased, as she always had, being honest with herself. If women were stupid enough to fall for her, that was their lookout.

She wasn't responsible for how other people felt, or reacted.

Inconsequentially, coffee popped into her thoughts, and she smiled to herself. "I always know when I've really hooked a woman, when she's really serious: it's the day she buys in my favourite blend of coffee! That's a sure sign of commitment, and usually a signal for me to wind things up with her!" Deftly negotiating a pothole, she chuckled. "One stupid cow even went as far as buying a coffee grinder and beans for me! That was time for a sharp exit on my part. I wonder if she sold the grinder on EBay, or kept it for her next girlfriend, like some kind of flawed talisman? What was her name again? Suzie? Sarah? God, I can't even remember… she had red hair and freckles, and coffee, of course…"

Frankie.
Her thoughts turned abruptly to Frankie, and that stolen kiss in the barn, only a few days earlier…

***

Frankie stared at herself in the mirror in her bathroom and examined the woman looking back at her. She saw an ashen, stricken face with frightened eyes and a forehead crumpled in dismay.

Feeling physically sick, she retched over the wash hand basin, watched from the doorway by Misty.

The cat was used to drama, living as she did with Frankie, and she sensed another episode was about to unfold. She turned away and washed her face with a paw, then slowly made her way downstairs to her basket, where she curled up for sleep again.

Upstairs, Frankie washed her face with cold water as the inner turmoil and guilt began. What had she done? It had all happened so quickly, she still didn't quite believe what had just happened in the barn. There were no excuses whatsoever, though. None at all…

She and Sam had been setting out the barn for one of the occasional communal meals the women ate together. They'd been laying oilcloth covers along two trestle tables and fixing them in place with blue tack, underneath the table tops.

Their fingers brushed as they smoothed out the cloth, and Sam suddenly grasped her hand, holding it gently but firmly.

"I should have pulled my hand away, instantly!" Frankie groaned. Sam, holding Frankie's gaze with her beautiful eyes, raised the other woman's hand to her lips and kissed it, before releasing her grasp. Carefully and slowly, she then tilted Frankie's chin upwards, and holding her face in both hands, kissed her with exquisite tenderness and a rising undercurrent of passion.

Mesmerised, Frankie's instincts overruled her head and her brain, and she kissed Sam back with equal force for several long minutes. Only when Sam's hand slid down her shirt and caressed her breast did she pull away, flushed and breathless.

"I, I can't do this, Sam!" she croaked, snatching up her jacket and backing towards the barn door, flinging it open and rushing out into the courtyard towards her cottage.

Sam said nothing to the fleeing Frankie, but smiled to herself and a few minutes later, let herself out of the barn, carefully securing the door shut. The wind and snow was picking up again and they had to make sure the barn stayed securely shut against the weather.

As she walked the few yards back to Horseshoes, Sam turned and looked up at the farmhouse. There at her study window was Jennifer, who couldn't have failed to see Frankie rushing homewards, her jacket open and scarf flying out behind her.

Sam halted for a few seconds and stared straight at Jennifer, who was watching, her face still. Sam smirked. Still holding Jennifer's gaze, she gave a small thumbs up sign, then slowly turned around, walking towards her cottage.

In Meadowfields, Frankie had poured herself a large gin.

She'd cheated on Jennifer, the woman she loved, with Sam, this sexy, charismatic woman who come among them. Sam was a player, that had been obvious from the start, she knew that, so why did she let that happen?

"Oh my god, how can I face Jen?" Frankie ground her teeth in guilt and desperation. There was nothing else for it. Cheating is cheating, whether it's a kiss, a fumble, a one night stand or a full blown affair, it's cheating. End of.

Her thoughts raced and tumbled as she glugged down the gin. "I'll just have to tell Jennifer what happened and take the consequences. I can't risk Sam telling her, or Jennifer finding out some other way. I wouldn't be able to hide it from her either, and even if I could, I don't want to: there would always be the guilt and the secret between us, how could we go forward from that? Johnny was arriving from Edinburgh next week, too, and looking forward to meeting Jennifer... the timing couldn't be worse."

"Well, Misty, this time, I've only myself to blame," she told the unconcerned cat. "If I lose Jennifer, this lovely woman who cares for me so much and has shown me nothing but kindness and love, then it'll be my fault and that'll be exactly what I deserve."

Chapter 14
A Confession

"I need to see you tonight, it's really urgent. Can I come over about 7-ish? Love you, F xx".
The text had pinged onto Jennifer's private iPad as she worked on a presentation for one of her clients. The calculations weren't going well, the figures were tumbling around, refusing to co-operate.

Jennifer braced herself for Frankie's visit, her stomach churning in that ghastly, washing machine spinning way which most people experience in times of anxiety and stress.
"If only I hadn't been sitting at the window, I'd be none the wiser," Jen's thoughts hurled around as her mood fluctuated from optimism to despair. "If only I hadn't been stupid enough to let myself fall in love with her! It's just setting myself up to be hurt, yet again!"

Jen closed down her work computer. There was no point in trying to do anymore today, she might as well give up. She replied briefly to Frankie's text, saying she's see her after 7pm. Two kisses at the end, but no declaration of love. Time to start building the barricades again, just in case things went wrong.

She'd spent a long time, after Vanessa, building up layers of bubble wrap, protecting herself from true involvement and possible hurt, and now, just as she'd let Frankie into her life, into her heart, and started dismantling the protection around her, it looked like she was about to be destroyed all over again.

Later that day, she answered Frankie's knock at the door promptly. Whatever was going to happen next between them, it was too cold to play childish games and leave the woman standing outside. Once in the hall, Frankie didn't even wait to take off her coat before bursting into tears.

"I'm so, so sorry, Jen! It didn't mean anything, honestly, but, I kissed Sam in the barn... well, she kissed me first but I didn't stop her, and I kissed her back, that was all, nothing else, oh god, how could I have betrayed you like that?"

She slumped down onto the chair in the hall and covered her face with her hands. She wasn't wearing gloves, and her skin had turned red with cold, even in the few minutes she'd been outside in the biting wind.

Jen's heart lurched with pity and love at the vulnerability of her lover, but she retained her outward composure. "Take off your coat and come into the warmth," she said, with only the slightest tremble in her voice. She poured Frankie a large glass of wine and gestured to the fireside chair.

Frankie took a large slug of wine and looked Jen in the eye. In a calmer voice she said: "I'm really, truly sorry, Jen. It's made me realise just how much you do mean to me, and how I'd hate to lose you… it was an insane, moment of madness, I should have stopped it right away."

Jen let a pause develop before she spoke, and when she did, she appeared calm, cool even. "Frankie, we both know what Sam is: a player. It's all just a game to her. She'd casually break us up, have a bit of fun with you, and then dump you as soon as the novelty wore off. My question is, have you got feelings for her, and if that's the case, do you want to end it with me and take a chance with Sam?"

Frankie stared at her. "No, of course I don't want us to end, Jen! You're a lovely woman, kind, good company, smart, sexy and funny and I truly love you, properly. I can't imagine not being with you now, and yes, I know what kind of woman Sam is, I've met the type before. She's just so charismatic, and she is beautiful, I got swept away, just for a few moments, but I know it was just so wrong. Maybe I shouldn't have told you…" she trailed off and took another large mouthful of wine.

"If you hadn't told me, it would have sat between us, a horrible secret," said Jen. "It would have tainted our relationship and I would have known you were keeping it from me."

Frankie looked up, startled. "How would you have known?" she exclaimed.

Jennifer held her gaze. "I saw you running out of the barn, then Sam emerging a couple of minutes later. She looked up at my window, with a horrible leer of triumph and gave me a thumbs up sign."

Frankie gasped. "What!"

Jen looked away, and stared into the fire. "Like I say, she's a player, Frankie. A beautiful, talented, confident woman who can get anyone she wants, and she knows it. Right now, she fancies you, and it would be a little triumph for her to take you away from me, just like that. You'd be another notch on her bedpost, and I'll guarantee that before long, she'll scarcely remember your name!

"All I will say to you is that I've been cheated on in the past, more than once. I gave one woman not just a second chance, but several chances, several benefits of the doubt. She betrayed my trust, endlessly, and eventually my self-respect woke up and took charge, and I left her. It was dreadful, I loved her deeply in spite of her behaviour, so I had to walk away from the woman I cared for and had hoped to be with for the rest of my life: it just wasn't going to work any longer. I knew that I was worth more than to be treated like that.

"I won't be treated like that again, Frankie." A hardness entered her voice, a new edge. "If you want to be with me, that's great. I love you, but have no wish to control you, or to keep you with me out of a sense of guilt. You stay with me because you want to, no other reason. If you don't want me, and don't want to be with me, say so now and we'll end it. But if you stay with me, you have to be faithful to me. If you can't agree to that, we're done."

Jennifer rose and poured them each another glass of wine.

Frankie stared into the flames for a couple of minutes before looking at her partner. "I've told you about Marion, how much I loved her, how hurt I was that she wouldn't leave her husband and be with me, and why I had to leave Edinburgh and start a new life here.

"I've had time to recover, to reflect and to put all that into perspective. I was wrong in the first place to get involved with a married woman. It was never going to go well, but it was just simply wrong anyway. She wasn't free to be with me, I shouldn't have got so close and allowed myself to get into it. I loved her deeply, passionately and madly, the connection between us was palpable, it fizzed and burned between us like lightning, but it was also like some kind of virus, infecting me, damaging me, causing sense to leave me, and hurting Marion so much too. It really was a doomed relationship, with disaster written all over it, fatally flawed. I know that now, for sure, but it was so painful to part from her…"

Frankie broke off, and wiped tears from her eyes. Jennifer made to say something, but Frankie stopped her. "Please just let me finish," she pleaded.

"I know now what it's like to be with someone who can commit to me, love me without restraint and without conditions and restrictions. I love you most dearly, Jennifer, and it feels right. I won't cheat on you again, not ever. You have my word. I hope you can forgive me and that we can get past this stupid thing I did."

Jennifer put down her glass, and moved towards Frankie, folding her in her arms, then kissing her gently, then passionately. When they broke for air, Frankie said: "I think we should go public to the others. Sam had obviously guessed we were an item, but we might need to spell it out for the rest of our neighbours. What do you think?"

"Yes, a good idea," said Jen. "We'll do it soon, maybe at this weekend's barn supper?" She smiled at Frankie. "Now, why are we still sitting here when my bed is feet away? I'm finding it quite hard to concentrate on this conversation…"

On their way upstairs, they stopped on the half-landing for an embrace so intense that they were half-undressed by the time they made it to the bed. In the bedroom, hauling off her unbuttoned shirt, Jennifer thought, distractedly, that maybe Sam had done them an unexpected favour. She and Frankie had a proper conversation, they knew where they were and what they wanted. It was going to be alright.

Chapter 15
Johnny Visits

In Edinburgh, Johnny opened a couple of windows in the flat and breathed in the distinctive scent of Edinburgh's winter air. The coldness blended with the familiar urban smells: diesel fumes, smoke from the few remaining coal fires in the sandstone tenement flats, engine oil from the nearby railway siding and faint whiffs of food from the many coffee shops and greasy spoons in the area.

Hanging quietly in the cold air, there was still the faintest trace of hops, a ghostly reminder of the city's brewing history, now confined to a small number of craft breweries.

The smell of fermenting beer had embedded itself in the stonework of the flats and the garden boundary walls, leaching into the very fabric of the city.

In the street below, Johnny watched the bustle of pedestrians, the ebb and flow of traffic and heard the beeping of the crossing signal at the lights. He loved this city, where he'd been born and lived all his life, and which grounded his being.

He couldn't imagine living anywhere else, it was a fixed point, secure and solid, to compensate for the gaps in his knowledge, and one huge, unanswered question.

He sighed, and thought again about the questions which had been bobbing up to the surface of his consciousness more frequently in recent times.

Who was his biological mother? Was she still alive and if so, where was she? Why did she give him up for adoption? Did she think about him ever? Did he really want to meet her, even if that was possible?

All he knew about his early life was that he'd been born in an Edinburgh nursing home, long closed, to an unmarried, teenage girl who'd put him up for adoption immediately after his birth.

"I couldn't ask for better parents than mum and dad," he thought. "They gave me a great childhood, lots of love and every opportunity. I just wish they'd been more forthcoming about my birth mother…I so wish I had asked, and found some answers!"

Sadness overwhelmed him for a moment as he thought about his parents. Already in their early forties when they adopted Johnny, calling time on their lengthy, fruitless efforts to conceive their own baby, they had taken him into their home and their hearts. His dad, Tom, had died from an unexpected and massive heart attack only a few years after his retirement. His mum, Joan, had succumbed to dementia and was now in a nursing home. Long gone were the days when he could have had an answer from her to his questions about his birth mother.

"Well, my son, you need to decide if you want to find out about the woman who gave birth to you or not!" He spoke out loud in the empty room, a habit he'd developed since Frankie and Misty left. "I miss you, Frankie," he muttered. "Who's going to help me decide about my mother and what I should do now. Do I plunge ahead and try to find her, which might be tricky, or do I leave sleeping dogs alone?"

Restlessly, he paced the pristine rooms of the flat. Although Frankie's untidiness had driven him crazy at times, and they squabbled over what she called his OCD and he called her sluttish behaviour, he missed the homely clutter she created more than he ever expected to do. "I guess I should look for another flatmate to share the bills meantime," he pondered, "at least until I find a place to buy. It seems the grownup thing to do, I suppose. The time has surely arrived for me to leave student life and flat-sharing behind."

He plumped himself down on the couch and flicked open a design magazine, flinging it down impatiently a few minutes later. Reaching for his phone, he tapped in Frankie's number. Decision time: he was going to visit her, check out her cottage, reconnect with Misty and meet this woman Jennifer she kept mentioning.

"Hi honey, it's your bestie. I'm getting the train today. No, not the Midnight Train to Georgia, good one, Frankie... Can you meet me at Dundee? Ok, I'll text you times, just going to fling some things in a bag."

He laughed. "Yes, obviously I'll bring wine, what do you take me for? Yeah, ok, I've time to nip up to Valvona & Crollas, text me a list...no Frankie, I'm not going to TKMaxx , you can go there yourself next time you're here...yes, I'll bring warm clothes, it's cold here too... now, I'm saying cheerio, see you tonight!"

He ended the call, and quickly packed a small case. Unhooking his coat and sticking a pair of gloves in the pockets, he added a beanie hat and scarf to his case. Glancing round the flat, he picked up the magazine he'd dropped on the floor earlier, and chuckling to himself, placed it tidily in the magazine rack.

Minutes later, he was downstairs and onto the street, heading purposefully up London Road towards the Italian delicatessen. As he walked along the busy street, he checked the train timetable on his 'phone.

Some hours later, he walked up to the concourse of Dundee train station to find Frankie, swathed in a bulky coat and huge scarf, waiting for him. Hugging each other warmly, and smiling from ear to ear, they looked at each other.

"I've missed you!" they both said at once, then burst out laughing.

"Come on," said Frankie, "let's head for the car and then home. The roads aren't great, but I'm getting used to driving in dodgy conditions!"

Less than an hour later, they were sitting before a crackling fire in Frankie's cottage, listening to the wind howling outside.

"This really is the back of beyond," Johnny observed, cupping his hands round a mug of tea. "What do you do for fun round here?"

Frankie gave a low laugh. "You'd be surprised how much entertainment there is round here. Just wait till you meet the neighbours…"

To Johnny's surprise, the woman stopped in mid-sentence and shifted uncomfortably in her chair.

"Ok, lady, give! What's happened? Does this call for wine?" Johnny rose and poured two hefty glasses of Merlot from the bottle breathing on a side table.

Hesitant at first, but with growing speed, Frankie told him about Jennifer – "You'll just adore her, Johnny, she's so sweet and lovely, and so kind to me!" – and then confessed her 'moment in the barn' with Sam.

"I've told Jen and she's forgiven me, but I know she won't forget and I need to work hard to regain her trust, Johnny. I really love her, you know, not in that stupid, crazy way I loved Marion, I was literally insane with love, I know that now. Jennifer and have something different. It's great, we really love each other, we have fun and it's pretty damn good between the sheets…" she broke off, seeing Johnny wince.

"Ok, I'll spare you the details," she laughed, "but it's like, I dunno, because we took time, got to know each other first, learned about each other's interests, ways of looking at the world, heard our back stories, we built something from the ground up. Different from some of the plunging headlong I've done in the past!"

She smiled ruefully. "You know what I mean, we've both done it!"

Johnny looked at her. "So, if it was so great, why did you jeopardise it with this Sam woman?"

Frankie stared at the fire. "I can't tell you, Johnny. It was just an insane moment of madness, a kiss out of nowhere from this massively attractive, charismatic woman. Once you've met Sam, you'll get it. I nearly lost Jennifer over this, and I'm making damn sure I steer as clear of her as I can. She'll be leaving in a couple of months, going back to Glasgow, so I can pretty much avoid her till she goes. When we do have to meet, I'll be polite but only say the bare minimum to her, it's the safest way.

"The others may suspect something has happened, but they're all too caught up in their own stuff to bother too much." She reached into the fireside basket and, opening the door of the wood burner, added another fragrant apple log to the flames. "Time I got the dinner going," she said. "Let's have a cosy night together and you can give me all the gossip from Edinburgh, including what's going on with your love life, you've been very silent on that in your texts." She hugged him briefly, then added: "Tomorrow, we're having lunch with Jen at the farmhouse, so I want you on your best behaviour! She's a neat freak like you, so be sure to take your boots off in the porch and no chucking coats and scarves around! "

Johnny relaxed in his chair, stroking Misty, who'd climbed into his lap, and chatted while Frankie made dinner. Contentedly, they fell back into their easy companionship, happy to be together again.

Misty's ears flicked now and then as she sensed the noises and murmurings from the walls, but she soon fell asleep again. Johnny was here, and her mistress was happy and safe. That's all that mattered.

***

"Come on Johnny, your hair looks fine! Stop preening and let's get over to Jen's!" Frankie reached for her coat and boots: it was still snowing and too deep for shoes. Johnny turned from the mirror and stuck the comb in his jacket pocket. "You take the wine and I'll bring the cheese, that should get me in her good books," he smiled. "Come on then!"

In the farmhouse, Jennifer stood at the sitting room window, watching for the pair emerging from Meadowfield. The casserole was simmering, the table had been laid with shining silver cutlery and sparkling glassware. The woman picked her thumbnail, acknowledging her tension. This was a big deal. Johnny was a major influence on Frankie, and if he didn't like her, that was going to be a problem.

She caught movement as the door of Meadowfields opened and Frankie and Johnny came outside, laughing at a shared joke. Jennifer watched them walk carefully through the snow. The man lifted his head so she had a full view of his face. Trembling, Jennifer clutched the back of a chair, her legs buckling under her and a drenching cold sweat pouring through her.

Adrian. He was the absolute double of Adrian, the same smile, jut of his chin, colour of hair, even the same slightly ungainly, loping walk. The years dropped away and she seemed to see her teenage boyfriend right there, in the flesh, older of course, but undoubtedly a carbon copy of the boy she'd known and loved.

With seconds to recover before her door knocker sounded, Jennifer called up an old trick of jettisoning herself into a safe space. She touched the curtain, the frame of a painting, the mantelpiece, looked at the rug, the snow outside, smelled the casserole and the pot pourri, fragrant in a glass bowl on the hall table; heard the faint hum of the freezer and the background music from the sitting room. She was calm as she opened the door, greeted Frankie with a warm hug and kiss and shook hands politely with Johnny.

There was then a bustle of coats being hung and boots stowed, and exclamations of thanks for the wine and cheese. Jennifer showed them to the fire, poured drinks and smiling, excused herself. "I'll not be a minute, just need to check on the food," she said, heading into the kitchen.

It couldn't be, could it? He was the right age, right location. Jennifer took a number of deep breaths and put herself back into work mode. She needed to process all this, not jump to silly conclusions, and find out more, much more. Maybe she was just over-wrought at the moment, what with Frankie and the Sam incident, and the awful vulnerability she felt, being in love and feeling her barriers coming down, knowing how exposed she now was to hurt and disappointment, after her careful distancing from entanglements in recent years. "Knowledge is power," she whispered to herself, stirring the casserole. "Facts first, speculation second!"

The lunch passed well, they all soon relaxed and chatted easily. Frankie and Jennifer regaled Johnny with tales of Barleyknowe and in turn, he was both interested and amusing company.

"You're a great cook, Jennifer!" said Johnny as he took the offered second helping of pudding. "That was fabulous!"

The talk drifted into other areas, and over coffee at the fireside, Jennifer asked Johnny, casually, about his family.

"Well," he said, stretching his feet towards the fire, "there's a story here, if you'd like to hear it?"

Jennifer nodded. "Only if you want to tell it, Johnny."

He glanced first at Frankie, then looked into the red cave of the fire. "I was born in Edinburgh, in a nursing home, to a very young mum. She was still at school and her boyfriend, my dad, was not much older. I know the date and place of my birth and my mother's name, but I've never made any efforts to trace her. I was adopted as an infant and my mum and dad gave me the best life, lots of affection and attention. They'd tried for a baby for years, apparently, but without any luck, so I had no brothers or sisters, but my parents encouraged me to make friends and bring my pals round to play. Can't say I ever felt lonely!"

He smiled. "Considering they were older parents with conservative views, they were brilliant when I came out as gay, well, bisexual, but hey, do we need labels?"

Frankie laughed, but she noticed Jennifer's knuckles were white as they gripped her coffee mug, and there was an odd tenseness about her. She turned back to listen to Johnny, but made a mental note to talk to Jen later. What could be wrong?

Johnny continued: "Frankie's probably told you how we met at college and became best buddies. Weird, actually, that Frankie and I have a similar story with teenage parents, I sometimes think that why we got along so well from the start.

"You know about Frankie's parents and the tragedy there, and how her aunt brought her up so well. We were both lucky to have caring people to raise us, I guess. Now my dad is dead and mum has dementia, I have been thinking about trying to find my biological mother, try to find out why she couldn't work out a way to keep me, get some answers as to why her family couldn't give her support."

"Excuse me a moment, I'll be right back." Jennifer rose to her feet swiftly and headed for the door. With a lover's insight, Frankie saw Jen's fleeting, stricken expression and heard the faintest moan from her throat. Or maybe that noise was just the wind wailing faintly down the chimney? Jennifer came back into the room a few minutes later, looking composed, and sat back down at the fireside. "What drew you to study art, Johnny?" she asked, smoothly and with real interest in her voice.

"Don't know, really, I was just always good at it, that and designing things," he answered. "One of the many things I don't know is if either of my parents was artistic, maybe it's in the genes?" He smiled. "Not that it matters all that much, really. We all get talents, and we use or lose them, don't we?"

Frankie glanced across at Jennifer again. What the hell was wrong? She was being polite and friendly, but it appeared as if she was making an enormous effort to keep control. Her smile was taut and her eyes showed veiled panic.

"I think we should be going back over to mine soon, honey," she said to Johnny. "I've still a lot of catching up to do with you before you head back to Auld Reekie tomorrow. We'll have an early night and I'll drive you to catch the red eye train from Dundee. You'll be in your office glugging back coffee by nine am!"

"Oh god, don't remind me, I've got work tomorrow! I feel so relaxed and at home here, I don't want to go back! And red eye only applies to planes, dopey!"

"Right, that's it, mister!" Frankie laughed. "You can bring in the logs tonight, in all that wind and snow!"

They left, the open door bringing in the darkening afternoon and the cold, primitive feel of snowy air. "It's been lovely to meet you, Jen," Johnny hugged her. "I feel much happier knowing Frankie's with such a lovely lady!" Frankie kissed her, murmuring: "Thank you, sweetheart. I knew you and Johnny would hit it off!" Leaning in, she whispered, "I'll be over tomorrow night" and then moved away, leaving the faintest scent of Opium hanging in the air.

"This can't be happening. It's too bizarre for words, what are the chances?" Jennifer's jumbled thoughts tumbled around as, on autopilot, she walked into the kitchen and mechanically loaded the dishwasher.

Tomorrow, she was going to find out the truth, but her guts were saying what her brain could scarcely even start to process.

Johnny was the baby she gave up, with such bitter regret, all those years ago.

He was her son.

Chapter 16
Revelations

"What! You had a baby? Johnny's your, your... son? Are you sure?"

Frankie stared at Jennifer, who was pouring them each a glass of wine, her hand shaking as she tilted the bottle.

"I don't know for sure, Frankie, that's why I need to find out for definite before I talk to him. I just don't know how I'm going to even begin to have that conversation." Jen abruptly laid down the bottle and glass on the kitchen worktop and began to cry.

Folding the woman in her arms, Frankie soothed her lover.

"Now, it's all going to be fine, let's just stay calm. Sit down and we'll talk this through sensibly. Have a drink first!"

Through her tears, Jennifer managed a weak smile.

"You think red wine's the solution to everything, Frankie!"

"It's never failed me yet," Frankie retorted, sitting down in an armchair near the fire. "Now, let's hear it from the start, nice and slow."

Jennifer wiped her eyes, and began. "I was just 15, almost 16, when I got pregnant, still at school, going into fifth year, all set to do my Highers and then go on to university. Accountancy and business law!" she paused, smiling wistfully. "I was at a good state school in Edinburgh, and was doing well."

Frankie registered surprise. "Why did I think you were from London?" she asked. "Your accent's not Scottish!"

Jennifer smiled again. "Oh, I moved around a bit, Aberdeen for a while, but then London for many years. I must have picked up the accent, though the people in my office always said I sounded Scottish. Anyway, that's not important."

She moved a little in her chair, and as Johnny had done the previous day, stared into the fire. The flames licked round the logs, sending tongues of bright orange upwards. "Adrian was my first real boyfriend, a year above me at school, and as handsome at get out. All the girls were after him, but he chose me. I couldn't believe it! Every time I'd seen him, in the art room or the dinner hall, I got tongue-tied and shy, and could hardly string a sentence together, but he must have liked something about me.

"I remember the very moment he asked me to go out with him. It was pouring with rain, a sudden heavy summer shower had just begun as we left school for the day. He caught up with me just outside the school gates, panting a little as he'd run across the playground. His blond hair was dark with rain, and his blazer already damp.

"He asked if I'd go to the pictures with him at the weekend, and I was surprised to see that his expression was anxious, as if he feared I'd say no."

She laughed again. "As if! He was the handsomest boy in the school, clever, and artistic too. I was truly smitten. We dated through till the end of term and into the next school year, and quite soon, things turned physical. We could scarcely keep our hands off one another… then there was the party at his friend's house… we had cider and beer, and everything went hazy. Next thing we were on his pal's bed, a hard, single one, I remember, and we were pushing coats onto the floor and hauling our clothes off."

Frankie cut in: "Don't tell me he didn't use a condom!"

Jennifer looked at her. "This was 35 years ago, Frankie. Things were different, and he was young too. He would have been way too embarrassed to go into a chemist and ask for condoms, besides, we didn't plan to have sex, it just happened!"

Frankie smiled ruefully. "Well, we've all been overwhelmed with lust and passion, I guess!"

Jennifer continued. "I just couldn't believe the bad luck that I was pregnant after having sex only once. At first I thought I was late, but I started being sick in the mornings, and my mother twigged on and hauled me off to the doctor."

Her face saddened and she sipped the wine. "The next months were like some hideous, protracted nightmare. Sometimes, in the morning as I woke, there were a few seconds when I forgot, but a kick from the baby soon reminded me that this was all real and dreadful.

"The two sets of parents met, along with me and Adrian, and our futures were laid out, with no quibbling allowed from either of us. Both mothers looked quite devastated, ashamed and embarrassed and our dads didn't make eye contact with either of us during that painful half hour.

"Adrian said nothing, but stared down at the carpet so intently, you'd think he was counting the flowers in the pattern!

"It was decided that I should stay at school meantime, then get home tutoring once the baby began to really show. Our headmaster was sympathetic, and arranged for me to sit my Highers in the May at an FE college exam centre where no-one knew me."

She looked at Frankie, who was listening intently, then added: "School staff would be told the situation on a need-to-know basis and the official line would be that I had an undisclosed illness which required a long convalescence. The baby was due in July, it would be adopted immediately, and I'd go back to school, into sixth year, as if nothing had happened. Adrian was due to leave school in the summer anyway, and he'd be off to university in the autumn."

Frankie took Jennifer's hands in hers. "That's brutal! Didn't you even have a choice about keeping the baby? Surely something could have been worked out..." she tailed off as she watched Jennifer's face dissolve into tears again. "Oh honey, I'm sorry, it must have been a nightmare for you!"

Jennifer reached for a tissue and blew her nose. "It was beyond awful, but by this time, Adrian and I were drifting apart anyway. It was just a teenage romance, fuelled by lust and alcohol that night. I doubt we would have stayed the course, especially when we went off to university.

" Even if we'd stayed together, we couldn't have supported a child. I knew it was the best, well, the only thing to do, for the baby's sake as well as ours. I never saw him again after that night, to speak to privately anyway. We avoided each other as much as possible when we were at school, looking the other way if we happened to meet in the corridor. It was dreadful, so sad."

She gazed at the fire. "Adrian went to university, to study architecture, but he didn't stay in touch with me. I expect my mother told his parents that the baby had been born and adopted, but it just wasn't discussed at home. I did look him up on Facebook a few years ago, just out of curiosity, and discovered he was living in Melbourne, seemed to be doing well, with his own firm, and married with two girls. I didn't contact him, what would be the point? Our lives went on different tracks a long time ago."

She glanced at Frankie, and saw tears glistening in her eyes. "I only saw my baby for a short while after he was born, the nurses let me hold him and say my goodbyes," she continued, a slight break in her voice. "He had these achingly exquisite, tiny finger nails and small red feet sticking out the bottom of his wee flannel nightie. I told him that I loved him so much, and wished with all my heart that I could keep him, but I couldn't. I was 16, a schoolgirl with no money and my parents wouldn't entertain the idea of an illegitimate grandchild.

"I cried and cried when the nurse took him away, there was an actual pain where my heart is, I truly thought it was broken. Maybe it was? I sometimes wonder if that all healed up properly! He was taken off to a foster home for a few weeks – that's what happened back then – and then adopted by his new parents. I left a letter for him, for his new parents to give him one day, saying how much I loved him and that I'd never forget him. I don't know if he ever saw the letter."

She started crying again. "Nothing since has ever been as hard as giving away my baby that day. If only things had been different, easier…"

Frankie sat silently for a moment. "Why do you think Johnny is your son?"

Jen answered slowly. "Firstly, he's almost a carbon copy of Adrian, right down to the walk and his laugh and his smile. He's about the right age and was born in Edinburgh to a single, teenage mum. When's his birthday?"

"The 15th of July, St Swithin's Day," Frankie said immediately. "We always check the weather forecast a few days beforehand. The legend goes that if it rains on St Swithin's Day, it'll rain for the next 40 days."

Jennifer looked at her: "That was the day my baby was born. One of the midwives looked out of the window and commented on the downpour, saying much what you've done. Do you know where Johnny was born, by any chance?"

"As a matter of fact, I do," said Frankie. "We'd been out walking one day and on the way home, as we headed back to our flat, he pointed to a large, stone house with a B & B board outside, and mentioned that had been a nursing home once and was where he'd been born. It was called The Birches, or something like that."

"The Beeches," said Jennifer. "Yes, that's it, The Beeches. Up in Newington somewhere," Frankie confirmed.
The two women stared at each other.

"We'll have to double-check, of course," said Jennifer after a minute. "I want to be absolutely sure before I even begin to figure out what, if anything, I'm going to do as regards telling Johnny. A lot has to sink in here, so please say nothing to him just now, Frankie."

Frankie looked as if she might protest, but thought better of it and agreed to keep quiet meantime. In silence, they sat at either side of the fire, each wrapped in thought.

Chapter 17
Tensions Rise

Rose watched her relationship deteriorate as Irene fell more under Sam's spell.

Their lovemaking became perfunctory, dutiful, a relief to be done with, so they could turn over and fall asleep.

They had always thought of their attraction as chemical, like two test tubes of blue liquid, bubbling and fizzing in the school science labs of their school days, before health and safety rules banished the flaring Bunsen burners from the classrooms.

Being around the same age, they remembered the wooden benches, hacked and scarred by penknives and the sickly, rotten egg smell which hung in a miasma around the lab.

In bed, at first, in those ecstatic early days, there had been passion, mutual satisfaction and love. "The right word for it now is definitely perfunctory," thought Rose, as she washed the dishes. "Brisk. Her body is still there when we have sex, but not her mind, or her emotions: they're missing. We simply lack excitement, we're boring each other rigid! And now this bloody woman has pitched up, at just the wrong time for us." She banged an angry pan on the draining board, crashing it down so hard that Irene looked up from the jersey she was knitting, but said nothing.

They sat having a cup of tea one evening, after a day in the garden. Irene sat looking into the fire, a TV guide drooping from her hands.

"What's on tonight, then?" Rose asked, a new brittleness about her voice.
"Oh, the usual for a Sunday, Antiques Roadshow, Call the Midwife, unless you want to watch Hoarders?" Irene replied, not looking at her. "Or, there's a repeat of Gardeners World, if you want to see that?"

"There's such a lovely cluster of miniature daffodils, just through in… quite a few of the gardens around." Irene's train of thought moved swiftly onto a different track, noticed instantly by Rose. Sam had a great show of early daffodils, brightening the small garden at the front of the guest cottages.

This was a new thing, Rose felt with a sickening thud in her stomach: Irene switching and diverting her speech away in mid-conversation, an abrupt backtracking, recovering of the safer position, drawing her dangerous thoughts back into a bunker. Rose's jaw hardened, and the slight ache reminded her that she was grinding her teeth again, something which last happened in her final year of teaching, when everything began to fall apart.

"I can't be jealous of flowers," Rose's thoughts tumbled around behind her blank expression. So typical, though, that Sam had managed to coax into being a slew of tiny bright yellow daffodils, the first of the season, despite the early frosts, sudden, unexpected snow storms and unforgiving winds of spring. Rose had been wheeling a barrow-load of garden debris to the communal compost heap when she'd spotted them, and had to look away.

Rose looked at Irene, who was still gazing into the fire, her mug of tea idle in her hand. They'd been through so much to be together, Rose reflected. There had been all that trouble with her husband and the divorce, and the problems trying to see her daughter, then the awful business at school, when things seemed at the time almost impossible to put right.

They'd persevered through it all, building a solid, lasting relationship amongst the storms and tempests of the couplings and uncouplings around them, and finally having the chance to lead the lives they wanted, here in this idyllic spot.

It's true that things weren't always perfect over this last couple of years, even before they moved to Barleyknowe, Rose admitted to herself. There were tiffs, arguments and downright rows sometimes – Irene could be volatile and bad-tempered, especially when she'd had a drink or two. All this led to cold-shouldering in bed, but underneath everything, they loved each other, they had a history, a present and a future together. Life should be good, and it usually was good. Apart from the situation with Katherine, of course…

Until Sam came along, that is. Rose put down the cup with an unnecessary jarring clatter. "Yes, I saw the display outside Sam's house," said Rose, that odd, tense note souring her speech. "She's certainly got green fingers, I'll give you that. It's just a pity she's so bossy!"

Irene looked up, her eyes wary and alert to the altered tone.

"Well, she always knows best, doesn't she?" Rose's words were tiny bullets ricocheting round the room. "She seems to know best about everything: gardening, cooking, music, current affairs, not to mention painting!"

There was a silence, as both of them thought of Sam, with her casual blonde hair flicked away from her pixie face, her huge blue eyes set wide and sparkling, and all the while, exuding that inner confidence which is so good to possess and often ghastly to behold.

The fire burned low, and Irene reached into a wicker basket for a seasoned apple log, which sparked as it caught ablaze. As she dusted her hands of the fragments from the log, Irene continued to look into the red cavern of the fire. She said nothing in response to Rose's comments, but her thoughts churned.

She was hiding it from Rose as best she could, and trying so hard to deny it to herself, bending her will, using her head not her heart, but it was unmistakable, without any doubt, she had fallen, and fallen hard, for Sam.

***

A week later, Irene sat alone in Glen View, nursing a whisky glass, staring unseeingly into the fire, her thoughts tumbling around her brain like some ghastly kaleidoscope. She'd closed the curtains against the dark night.

Winter had reluctantly given way to a weak, faltering spring, and although the Angus countryside was still buffeted at times by sharp winds, the days were slowly lengthening and stretching their weary fingers outwards.

A pale, watery sun shone at times, and more spring flowers emerged from their hiding places in the damp earth. Irene sighed heavily, and took a slug of whisky.

This week was her time to think, and think hard, what she should do about Rose, and about Sam. Rose had taken advantage of her improved health and better weather to visit Katherine and her family in Glasgow. "I'll be off then," Rose had said, briskly clipping shut her suitcase and heading for the door. "See you in a week," she added, pulling on gloves and turning her head so that Irene's parting kiss grazed her cheek.

She closed the door quietly but firmly, without a backward glance at her partner, the rage, hurt and disappointment she felt bubbling up inside her afresh. A week apart would do them both the world of good.

Irene placed another log on the fire. The radio burbled in the background, tuned as usual to classic FM which they both loved.

"We've so much in common, been through such a lot just to get here, to this point and place in our lives," Irene thought sadly, sipping her whisky. Sam. Was she the cause of their unhappiness, or just the catalyst, the bucketful of cold water flung over them to show the flaws and imperfections in their relationship?

There was no doubt that Rose irritated her at times, Irene ruefully recognised. "I expect Rose has plenty to find fault with in me too," she thought.

Sam. Her thoughts kept coming back to this charismatic, sexy young woman, who'd awakened feelings in her which were terrifying, exciting and overwhelming. "Stop being so stupid, Irene!" She spoke out loud to the empty room, the words breaking the peaceful mood. "She's just having some fun with you, her heart isn't engaged, and you know she be off back to her real life in Glasgow soon, leaving you desolate. Rose knows already that there's something up, how will I be able to pretend once Sam goes?

Sighing, she went into the kitchen and began making a Spanish omelette for supper. Just as she was about to slide the food onto a plate, she heard a faint tap at the back door, and Sam quietly let herself into the room.

She said nothing, just held Irene's gaze and slowly took off all her clothes, leaving on only her green silk bra and pants. Smiling, and never moving her eyes from Irene's, she walked over slowly and took the pan from Irene's hand, setting it carefully on the trivet.

"If you're hungry later, I'll make you another omelette," she whispered, pulling Irene into her arms. With satisfaction, she heard Irene's low moan of pleasure and felt the woman's body respond to hers as she kissed her slow and long.

Later, they sat up in the spare room bed having a cup of tea. Irene had drawn the line at them having sex in what she called the 'matrimonial bed'. At the time, Sam had chuckled inwardly, but gone along with Irene's scruples.

Sam glanced sideways and caught Irene's expression. She saw, in those seconds, devotion, lust, infatuation and neediness all rolled into one on the woman's face. She sighed inwardly. Irene was well aware of the situation, Sam had spelled it out clearly right at the start. "I'm not up for long-term involvement or serious relationship here, Irene, this is just a bit of fun, an interlude in your normal life, if you like. You're with Rose, I know that, and I don't want to mess things up for you and her." Irene has acquiesced, agreed to Sam's blunt conditions, but looking back, maybe she hoped for more? Too bad, thought Sam.

Sam smiled at Irene, and turning back, drained her cup. "Would you like some more tea?" Irene asked.

"I wouldn't say no to a coffee, if that's no bother?" Sam replied calmly, as Irene jumped out of bed, her own drink cooling on the bedside table, and flung on her dressing gown. Sam watched Irene scurrying out of the room and patter downstairs to make coffee.

Coolly, Sam stretched out her long, lovely legs under the duvet. "This has definitely gone on long enough," she thought. "She's really fallen for me and what should have been just a bit of fun is about to turn into a giant pain in the arse. I can see it coming, clear as day!"

Composing herself as she heard Irene returning, a little breathlessly, upstairs with a tray. On it were two cups, a cafetiere, milk in a little jug and a plate of croissants with a pat of butter in a dish. The tray was completed with an artificial rose.

"Sorry there are no real roses at this time of year," Irene apologised, plunging the coffee and pouring Sam a cup.

"No problem," Sam said, accepting the cup.

The women chatted as they ate and drank. "When's Rose returning?" Sam asked, buttering a second croissant.

She felt Irene stiffen slightly next to her, and her voice held strain as she replied: "She'll be home on Saturday or Sunday, I think. She hasn't been in touch except for a text to say she'd arrived safely. I expect she's busy with her daughter and the family." Sam put down her cup and turned to face the older woman.

"Irene, we've had a lot of fun the past few weeks, haven't we?" Without waiting for an answer, she went on. "You're a lovely woman, and it's been great, but I think it's time we stopped seeing each other. Rose and you have been together a long time, you obviously love each other, and in any case, I'll be going back to Glasgow quite soon…"

She tailed off as Irene started to cry, quietly at first, but soon with huge sobs racking her body.

"Please don't say that, Sam! I love you so much, I'll leave Rose and come to Glasgow with you! I've been struggling with my feelings for weeks but I know for sure that I love you." The tears flowed unchecked down her cheeks.

"She looks so old, so haggard," thought Sam. "Why did I ever even go there?" If Irene had been one of her previous lovers, Sam would have been curt and brutal, but a tiny semblance of pity for Irene, and guilt for her own behaviour, intervened.

"I'm so sorry, Irene, but I don't feel the same about you. I don't want to be committed to you, as I told you right at the start. It's been good, but that's it. I certainly don't want you uprooting from your life here and following me to Glasgow. The last thing you should do is leave Rose, she's a nice woman who cares a lot for you, and you have a history and a good life together."

Sam hugged the weeping woman briefly, then rose from the bed. Unselfconscious in her naked beauty, she said: "It's time we went back to normal life again, Irene. This has just been an interlude, a bit of fun."

She hesitated at the bedroom door. "We'll be neighbours for a few more weeks till I leave, so let's just try and act normally when we meet with the others."

A minute later, putting on her scattered clothes in the sitting room, she heard Irene crying as if her heart would break.

***

Two doors up, in Springburn, the previous evening, Elaine and Archie were also preparing dinner.

He set the table and banked up the fire, pouring them each a glass of wine, while Elaine drained vegetables. Soon, they were eating the chicken casserole she'd served them, but there was a strained atmosphere hovering between them.

"What I can't understand is how Sam ever put two and two together and figured out that Jean was your wife? And what possessed her to tell Jean about us? What are we going to do now?"

Elaine gave up the pretence of eating and put down her fork, looking in fear and exasperation across the table at Archie.

He too was toying with his food. "This is lovely, Elaine, but I'm just not hungry," he said, looking at her, sadness pulling down the corners of his mouth. He took a mouthful of wine.

"I know now how it happened, I can explain that bit. Apparently, they were in the hairdressers in Forfar, in adjoining chairs, and got chatting while something set…" he tailed off.

Elaine smiled weakly. "They'd be waiting for the base colour to fix, I expect. Go on."

Archie looked around the room, as if searching for help of some kind, but not finding it, said: "Well, Sam said where she lived, Jean knew the farm, mentioned my name and said I played in the local hotel some nights.

Seemingly, Sam remembered that I was the man she'd seen at the hotel one day when she'd been there for lunch when I was playing, and realised it was me she'd also seen going into yours a couple of times. I thought I was being so careful too, avoiding being seen by any of your neighbours!"

Elaine said slowly: "I think I can explain that bit. One night I woke in the early hours, it was very windy and the bin blowing over wakened me. I was making a cup of tea when I noticed the lights on across at Horseshoes and saw Sam standing at the window, looking out into the night. I suspect she doesn't sleep well, and might have seen you walking up or down the lane one night."

She looked at Archie, and he saw a flash of anger in her eyes. "I think we've figured out the mechanics of this, but why she dropped you in it with Jean, I'll never understand. That's just malicious. I haven't done anything to her, as far as I know!"

"I've no idea, Elaine." He bowed his head. All of this was entirely his fault, and now he dragged Elaine, a perfectly lovely woman, into his mess. "I'm so sorry about this, it's my doing and I need to fix it."

"Archie! I went into this with you with my eyes wide open," she said quietly. "I knew that you were married, and I got on board with the situation. There was always a risk we'd be caught and that Jean would take it badly, we knew all this, and also that you were on your last warning. Well, it's happened, and we need to figure out what to do next."

She looked at him again, and underneath the anger and frustration which simmered in her eyes, he saw the tenderness and love she had for him. He swallowed hard to rid his throat of the lump he felt swelling there. He so loved this woman.

Archie's gaze travelled to where his suitcases sat near the door, buckled and bulging, silently reproachful, remembering the scene as they were dragged from a box room and filled with a jumble of clothes and toiletries. Jean watched him pack that night, and he was struck by her cold calmness.

When his past affairs had been discovered, she'd shouted and wept, raged at him and then not spoken to him for a few weeks, but had always forgiven him in the end.

This was different. Something had hardened in Jean, and, being honest, he didn't really blame her.

He looked at Elaine again. "There's no going back this time," he said." Jean's made it clear as day that she's had enough of me, wants what's left of her life to be peaceful and stress free, and above all, without me in it. I don't blame her, to be honest.

"Also, to be honest, I don't want to go back. I've had dalliances before, and I've told you about them, with no pride, only shame. But this is different, Elaine. I want to spend the rest of my life with you."

There was a long silence, then Elaine rose from her chair, came round to his side of the table, and cupping his wet cheeks in her slender hands, kissed him long and tenderly. They sat long into the night, talking and thinking, till finally Archie said: "I'm sorry sweetheart, but I have to turn in. I haven't slept much the last couple of nights and I'm just done in."

Elaine looked at him. "At least we know you can stay here for a bit," she reassured him. "Jennifer has been very understanding about the situation when I went to see her yesterday. She's ok about you living here with me as long as it's short-term. Long-term, it would be against the special clauses of the deeds, where permanent residents have to be women."

She smiled ruefully. "I never expected this turn of events," she said, "but we just have to figure something out longer-term." She smiled as he bent to kiss her goodnight.
"We'll sort all this out in the morning," she said. "I'll be up to bed soon."

She watched him leave the room, but made no move to follow him. Instead, she poured herself another drink and sat back down in her armchair. It was so long since she felt this angry, that the emotion felt huge and heavy in her head and heart.

The hand holding the wine glass tightened, the knuckles whitening as a slow, burning rage licked through her body: the kind of rage and frustration which had consumed her when she was with Billy, and which had been absent for so long now that she hadn't recognised it at first.

Her anger was not directed towards Jean. She didn't blame her for turfing Archie out at long last, she'd have done the same in her circumstances. In fact, she felt very sorry for Jean, and could only imagine the horrible humiliation she must have felt in the hairdressing salon that day. Others had heard and seen what happened as Jean threw off her gown, flung money onto the counter and stormed out into the street, a towel still wrapped around her neck, to the stunned astonishment of the customers and staff.

She wasn't angry with Archie either, or herself. To some extent, they were getting their just desserts, and would now need to deal with the situation in the best and most dignified way they could manage, with the least hurt to Jean and themselves. It was increasingly inevitable that he and Jean would part at some point, but the control and timing had been swept away from them all by Sam's cruel and needless interference.

There would be dreadful times ahead, and she shrivelled inside at the thought of what Archie would need to go through soon: the anger and possible rejection by his children, the divorce, money issues, house move, local gossip and losses of all kinds.

She'd be there for him throughout, of that she was sure. A shudder of pure hatred rippled through her body again. "That bloody, bloody awful woman Sam! How dare she meddle like this!"

The wine glass finally broke, the pressure from her angry hand too much to bear. As she staunched her cut hand with a wad of tissues and rose to fetch a brush and pan, the burning anger was replaced by a cold, clear sense of purpose.

Revenge was a dish best served cold, and Elaine intended that Sam should pay for what she'd done. She was patient and could wait, but the chance would come, and she'd be ready.

Chapter 18
Maureen and Jo

This must be what it really does feel like to be happy, Maureen thought, checking the stitches she'd cast on to her knitting needles. Jo needed to keep her neck warm when she was working outside and she never seemed to have a scarf to wear. Well, she'd have one soon, a rainbow scarf!

It sometimes seemed like a dream, everything that had happened in the last few months since that night when Jo had told her that she loved her, but knew she was straight, so it couldn't ever be more than a friendship... Maureen had stopped her speech in the simplest possible way by kissing her firmly on the mouth.

"Of course I know you love me, you idiot!" she said when they finally paused for breath. "Didn't you guess that I loved you too?"

Jo had looked at her. "Are you sure, Maureen? You've not been with a woman, have you? How do you know?"

"I know what love is, Jo," she replied, smiling. "I've been in love before, a long time ago, it's true, but I haven't forgotten how it felt. I know for certain that I love you. Love is love, isn't that what they say these days?"

Jo still hesitated. "Maureen, but what about the physical side of this? Do you want me, well, that way?"

Maureen smiled and without speaking, took Jo's hand and led her to the bedroom, where, with exquisite tenderness and sensitivity, building to overwhelming passion, they made love throughout the winter night. The stars looked down on the little house, whose stones stirred in primitive remembrances. What else is there truly, but love, hate, fear, sex and death?

Pausing in her knitting, Maureen smiled as she recalled that first night, and the growing of their relationship since then.

"What you thinking? You're miles away!" Jo's voice startled her.

"I didn't hear you come in!" she said, laughing.

"I took my boots off out the back and crept in only wearing my socks, so I could catch you unawares," growled Jo, nuzzling her neck. "You want a cuppa? It's still cold out there but at least it's not dark so fast today."

Jo filled the kettle and took down two mugs. "You'll never guess what's happened! All those lovely early miniature daffs outside Sam's have been pulled up and thrown on the ground: and one of her tyres is flat. What do you make of that?" she asked, dropping teabags into the cups. Maureen put down her knitting.

"Who would have done such a thing?" she queried, a frown forming on her brow. "I don't like the sound of that, I feel so safe here!"

Jo put down the teacups. "Sam thinks there's a rational explanation and we shouldn't jump to conclusions. The flat is probably a slow puncture from a nail she's run over somewhere, and the daffodils were likely dug up by an animal, maybe a fox or squirrel, looking for food."

Maureen sipped her tea. "Maybe, Jo, but I don't like it. Some of Sam's washing disappeared from the line last week. She thought it had blown off in that fierce wind we had, but clothes don't usually disappear into thin air, they end up in someone else's garden or in a field!

"Then there was the missing parcel with her new paint brushes which the postman says he left in the unlocked back porch. And it's always Sam that's affected, no-one else has had a problem."

The two women sat in silence, drinking tea.

With a pang of conscience, Maureen recognised that she was actually enjoying Sam's annoying misfortunes. "She's an arrogant and self-centred young woman," she thought. "If someone is playing pranks on her, well, she's getting what she deserves!"

***

Outside Horseshoes, Sam angrily scooped fresh potting compost into her tubs, and pressed the daffodils back into place then watered them in.

"Most likely they're dead, and there's not much chance of them recovering," she muttered under her breath. "Who would do this? Why?" She flung down the trowel and headed for the cottage door.

Elsewhere at Barleyknowe, a curtain was carefully moved back into place and a watching figure retreated from the window, a satisfied smile curling their expression.

Chapter 19
Jennifer and Johnny

February 2012

"What are you going to do about Johnny?" she asked, not looking up at her partner.

Jennifer bit her lip. "I've got to choose my moment, Frankie. It isn't something you can just blurt out!"

"Yes, of course," said Frankie, "but you're pretty sure, aren't you? Now you've checked back the records of the old nursing home and the birth certificate at Register House, there's not really any doubt, is there? The only other baby born there the same week was a girl. It's got to be him."

She looked straight at Jennifer. "I understand you being cautious, but the longer this goes on, the more difficult I'm finding it, sweetheart. Johnny's my best friend and my soul mate. We tell each other everything, he saved me from going under when Marion ended it with me. I was suicidal, Jen, and he pulled me out of a very dark place. I feel uncomfortable with having this huge knowledge about his life, something he needs to know and doesn't know."

Jennifer's eyes filled with tears. "I know, I know," she whispered. "But what if he's angry with me for what happened, and wants nothing to do with me? No sooner do I find him than I lose him, and what if I lose you too? I know how close you two are, and it's wonderful, but he might turn his back on both of us, or on you, and I couldn't bear to be the cause of a rift between you…" She began to cry, great, gulping, odd sobs that came from deep inside her, rending out through her throat.

"Oh, darling," Frankie held her, wiping away her tears with her fingers. "It'll be fine. I know Johnny, he's a kind and sensitive man without a bad bone in his body. He'll understand why you had to have him adopted. You heard him, his parents gave him a great life and lots of love. He brought them great happiness and joy at a time when they'd all but given up hope of having a child."

Taking Jennifer's hand, she said: "You need a cup of tea and one of my famous foot rubs," she said.

***

Jennifer drew her Honda smoothly to a halt in the car park at Carnoustie, which overlooked the sea and was handy for the railway station. She could have driven to Edinburgh, or caught the train at Arbroath, but she felt the need of a few minutes at this seafront, gathering salt air into her lungs.

She walked along the sea front, admiring the periwinkle ice cream colours of the promenade, watching the foamy sea slide up and down the beach in ancient, rhythmic pulses, halted by the rocks and pulling back again.

The timeless, endless nature of the process was reassuring, giving Jennifer a few minutes of peace from the turmoil which had been tormenting her for weeks now.

Meeting Johnny had created a whole series of emotional and practical issues, layering onto the Johnny issue, as she mentally labelled it. "Should be the Frankie and Johnny issue," she thought ruefully. "The whole thing is so tangled, and only I can begin the unpicking process! Down to me, and it can' be delayed any longer, for Frankie's sake as well as my own sanity!"

Gathering up her handbag, she walked slowly to the station platform, and a few minutes later was on the train to Edinburgh.

A couple of hours later, she and Johnny were sitting in a pub on the Royal Mile, in a corner booth. "Before we order, just tell me everything is ok with Frankie," Johnny said, looking at her with Adrian's eyes.

Good grief, he even had the same expression, that slightly anxious cast, thought Jennifer, but she answered him calmly.
"Yes, she's ok, she's fine and enjoying life at Barleyknowe."
Johnny was silent for a moment, then asked: "Are things good between you?"

Jennifer smiled. "Yes, you can rest assured on that one! We're very happy. I love her deeply, Johnny, and she feels the same. We're considering what to do next, but there are other factors, which is why I wanted to meet with you alone today. Frankie knows I'm seeing you and why."

"Let's order some food, and I'll get us a drink, then we can talk properly," suggested Johnny.

For the next hour, they ate and talked, then Jennifer said: "There's no easy way to introduce this subject, Johnny, so I just have to lay out the facts before you. I expect you to be disbelieving, shocked, and angry even, but I hope you'll understand after a while."

Jennifer laid down her fork and sipped the mineral water, then began her story: how she and Adrian had been teenage lovers, how her parents wouldn't let her keep the baby she gave birth to in the nursing home; the adoption, her constant sadness and regret and then seeing him that day at Barleyknowe, the startling resemblance to Adrian and her investigations in the records office and about the nursing home.

Now and then Johnny gasped, but he listened attentively.

Jennifer looked at him, and with a catch in her voice, said: "Johnny, I'm certain you're my biological son," she said. "We can do a DNA test to confirm it of course, but the only other baby born at the nursing home that week was a girl.

"I look at you and I see Adrian, or the man he would become: I haven't actually seen him since he was 18!"

Johnny sat in silence for several minutes, fiddling with a beer mat, and looking down at the table. Jennifer too looked down, leaving the silence to thicken between them.

Eventually, Johnny spoke, and his voice was brittle and strained. "Does Frankie know?" he asked.

"Yes," said Jennifer, slowly. "She knew there was something troubling me after you visited and had lunch with me. I had to tell her, and she's been very uneasy keeping this to herself. Please don't be angry with her, Johnny, she's been incredibly torn about this situation.

"You know how much she cares for you! You can be as angry as you like with me: for giving you up in the first place, for not trying harder to keep you, or for telling you now, I expect all of that, or none of that, and I have no right to ask anything from you.

"I've met you as an adult, and was so glad to hear that your mum and dad gave you such a happy childhood. They sound great people, and I'm sad your dad has passed away and your mum is so ill with dementia. They've done a fantastic job raising you to the man you are, and I'm endlessly grateful that you were wanted and loved and cherished."

Jennifer stopped. "I need to visit the ladies. Would you like another drink?"

"Yes, thanks," said Johnny.

"I'll get it on the way back." Jennifer rose and headed for the cloakrooms, leaving the man to deal with the churning, bewildering thoughts tumbling through his head as he began what would be the long process of coming to terms with the revelations, reconfiguring his past, his present and now, his future.

***

"How did you leave it with him?" Frankie's anxiety was palpable. Jennifer poured a second glass of wine for each of them, and sat down heavily in her chair.

Frankie drew the curtains against the darkening evening.

"He was, is, very shocked, as I expected," said Jennifer, easing off her shoes. "We parted quite formally at Waverley Station, with only the briefest hug.

"He says he needs space and time to process everything, but feels we should have DNA testing to be absolutely sure. He doesn't disbelieve me, but I understand his caution. I'd be doing and feeling exactly the same in his position."

"Like mother, like son," smiled Frankie, then said, "Oh, I'm sorry, poor taste, eh?"

"He took a few strands of my hair for the test," Jennifer began, then broke off and began to cry. "He looked so sad, so confused, so absolutely stunned... then so cold and distant, icily polite!

"Maybe I should have let sleeping dogs lie, kept the secret! "

Her arms around her, Frankie soothed her lover. "He just needs time and space, Jen. I know him well, as well as one person can ever know another. Leave him be for a while." She sat on the floor at Jen's feet, her arm resting on the older woman's lap. "What you need is a relaxing bubble bath and an early night. You've had an exhausting day and done a big thing. Tomorrow is, as they say, another day She rose to her feet. "We'll discuss this tomorrow when you feel more rested."

"Transactional analysis," murmured Jennifer, sleepily. "Eh?" Frankie paused on her way to the door. "I'm the child today, and you're the mother," smiled Jennifer. "Now, go and run my bath, and light a few candles up there while you're at it. I plan to soak there for some time!"

***

Alone in his flat, Johnny sat on the settee, a cigarette burning in a saucer which served as an astray. He and Frankie had both stopped smoking before she moved to Barleyknowe, ridding the flat of ashtrays at the same time, but Lady Nicotine seemed the only realistic support tonight, as his thoughts churned and tumbled.

"Try talking out loud," said a voice deep his brain. "Let the thoughts come out into the air, give them substance, make them heard and understood, allow yourself to hear and feel everything."

Good advice from me to me, he thought, a faint smile drifting across his face. He stubbed out the cigarette and paced the sitting room, first grounding himself, a technique Frankie had shared from her counselling sessions.

"I see the kitchen table, the pin board, the clock, people in the street, rain falling. I hear the traffic, the hum of the fridge, faint music from downstairs. I feel the cushion, the newspaper, my scarf, this apple from the fruit bowl…"

He took several deep breaths, inhaling and exhaling, and began to talk. "I always knew I was adopted, so no surprises there for me. I knew where I was born, and the situation my mother was in when she became pregnant and gave birth to me. I loved my mum and dad, and had a happy childhood. These are all pluses.

"I love Frankie as a sister, and I like what I know of Jennifer. I think she'll treat Frankie properly and she clearly loves her. I want to see Frankie happy and settled with someone she loves and who is kind to her. If I'm honest, this part is good for me too: it lets me move out of the odd limbo I've been in where Frankie and I could be grown-up children together. This is all good so far.

"I understand why Jennifer had to give me up, even before I knew who my mother was, I understood that bit and didn't blame her. So what's the stumbling block?"

He lit another cigarette and watched the blue smoke curl upwards. "The stumbling block is that my best friend, my soul mate, Frankie, is in a serious relationship with my biological mother!"

Sitting down again, he tried to square the circle. "You know that Frankie is happy, and weird though all this is, it could be ok. I just need time to figure it all out, put some boundaries in place. Perhaps Frankie and I will lose a little of our closeness: there will be some things she won't discuss with me about Jennifer now she knows I'm her son, but we'll always love each other.

"Time's what I need, to settle all this in my head, to get to grips with the new normal, our new situation… and maybe it's high time I began my new life too. It was all too cosy with Frankie, it sheltered me from growing up properly, and that's what I need to begin to do!"

Shocked at his conclusions, Johnny sat as the silence thickened, gathering around and over him like a blanket. He felt the weight of the stillness and quiet, allowed himself to experience it, to sink down into it, to be calm.

This big thing had happened, so huge that it would take him days, months, maybe longer, to process it. "Let yourself off the hook, Johnny," he said to the familiar room. "Tomorrow's a new day, when you can send off the DNA test and settle any lingering doubts about Jennifer being your mother once and for all. Now, it's a pizza, a bottle of beer and bed for you, my lad!"

Chapter 20
Disaster

Two weeks later

"It's still too cold to do without the heaters," said Frankie, moving a trestle table into position in the barn, and pulling benches towards it.

"Yes," agreed Jennifer, unwrapping a large waxed tablecloth. "I'll come over and switch them on tomorrow morning so they've plenty of time to warm the place up before the meal."

"Good idea to use Ploughman's Rest for the cooking this time. It'll heat the place up a bit: it's months since anyone used it," Frankie said, pushing the second table into place.
"Well, you can't expect people to visit much at this time of year!" Jennifer retorted. "Everyone is waiting till the weather improves!"

Frankie laid cushions along the benches, pushing back her curls as she stood up again from her task. Jennifer paused to watch her, and felt the familiar pulsing lurch travelling through her body, desire, love, wonderment, affection and energy throbbing through her blood and bones. Sometimes it all felt too good to be true, that this beautiful woman loved her in return, it seemed impossibly wonderful...

"What are you thinking, you hussy?" Frankie was staring at her, smiling. "Let me guess..."

They both began laughing, and, tasks abandoned, fell into each other's arms.

"Enough of this," said Frankie, pulling away, still smiling. "There's work to do, lady!"

"It's pretty well organised," Jennifer replied. "Everyone is bringing a dish and drinks, and Rose has volunteered to come over early to Ploughman's Rest to heat up the oven and begin cooking the meat and baked potatoes. It's a shame that Irene's laid up with that throat infection and doesn't feel up to coming along. Rose can take her over a plateful of food, if she feels like eating, that is!"

The next morning saw a watery sun rise, generating a weak spring sunshine if little heat. Activity increased in the courtyard as the women walked to and fro between their own homes, Ploughman's Rest and the barn, which was gradually warming up as the heaters took effect.

Irene, fully dressed but with a thick scarf wound round her throat, sipped a hot lemon drink as Rose collected a bottle of wine, glasses and cutlery and lowered them into a large carrier bag.

"You stay cosy, Irene, keep the fire banked up. I'll bring you over some food: what do you feel you could manage? How about some leek and potato soup?" Rose's tone was civil but perfunctory. She could have been back in the classroom organising care for a sick child, though Irene. There's not a grain of warmth about her towards me these days. Surely she can't have guessed? She and Sam had been so careful, but Rose wasn't stupid…

"Thanks," she croaked. "Maybe bring me back some soup later."

"Ok." Rose carried her bag to the door, opened and closed it without a backward glance. Once outside, her facial expression slumped and, head bowed, she headed for the barn. A minute later, she began mechanically laying out cutlery and glasses while her thoughts tumbled around in a frenzied jumble.

If only, if only she didn't know, know for sure, but she did and couldn't undo the knowledge. It was such a simple thing too, finding that tiny, scribbled note when she was hoovering under the spare room bed the week before. "Under the bed! In our house, our home! While I was away, trying to mend fences with my own family, that utter bitch, those utter bitches, were fucking!"

Rose felt a wave of heat race through her. Swearing didn't come naturally to her, but that day, with that discovery, a torrent of bitter, angry and crude words burst out from her mouth, landing in the silent bedroom, leaving her shaken, horrified and distraught.

Irene had gone to Arbroath for groceries, leaving Rose to hoover and dust the cottage. The slip of paper had obviously fallen down the back of the bed and been trapped in a dust ball. "You're wonderful, darling Irene. Can't wait for the next time we get naked and I lick you all over again. Sam xxxx"

Rose had a couple of hours to compose her thoughts and her expression before Irene returned with the shopping. She burned the note on the fire: no need to keep any evidence, the words were burned into her brain forever. Over the following week, she contrived to stay out of Irene's way on various pretexts. She had to get some head space to clear and process her thoughts. Every now and then, a lick of pure hatred flicked through her, burning her body and making her breath come in short bursts. Hatred for Sam, and anger at Irene, filled her every waking moment, and made it almost impossible to act normally around Irene.

"This can't go on," she thought, laying out the glasses. "It simply can't go on. Irene isn't herself either, not just the bad throat, she's miserable and distracted. Love sick or torn with guilt, I don't care. The two-faced, two-timing rat! And as for that Sam…" Her inner dialogue faltered as Frankie came in to the barn, carefully shutting the door behind her.

"Hi Rose," she said. "Great to have some heat in here at last! It's been a long winter, hasn't it?" She inspected the table. "Yeah, that looks great, I reckon we've enough cutlery for everyone. How's Irene today?"

"Not very well," she answered neutrally. "She's up and dressed and sitting at the fire with a book of crosswords, but not fit to be over here for the meal. I'll pop back over with some food for her later."

"Mmmm, this smells wonderful!" Jennifer lifted the lid of the giant soup pot sitting on the range in Ploughman's Rest.

"Leek and potato soup, my mother's recipe," smiled Maureen.

Maureen smiles a lot these days, thought Jennifer with amusement.

"We'll all be glad of it today," she grinned back at Maureen. "It's still quite nippy and a bowl of soup is just the thing for a starter."

The small kitchen was soon bustling as the other women brought dishes of food to heat in the oven. "Sam's going to be a little late," Jennifer mentioned as they prepared to head towards the barn, Maureen and Jo carrying the soup pot between them. "She's just texted to say she's baking quiches at her own house and they aren't quite ready. She'll bring them through here in a bit to stay warm in the oven, and then come across to join us."

Soon all the women, except Irene and Sam, were taking their places in the barn and chatting as Maureen ladled out the soup.

"This is lovely," Archie said appreciatively, tasting the first mouthful. "My old mum used to make a fine pot of soup, but I have to say this is braw!"

The women all laughed. There had been a little trepidation when they all read Jennifer's text earlier that day, explaining Elaine had Archie be living with her temporarily and she hoped none of the women minded this arrangement as she was aware it broke the conditions of sale. After thought, though, they had all texted Jennifer back to say they didn't object to Archie being among them meantime.

"I'll just pop over with some soup for Irene," said Rose, rising from her place and ladling a couple of scoops into a chunky earthenware bowl. She covered the bowl with a tea towel and walked carefully out of the barn door, which Archie held open for her.

Outside her own house a few moments later, she carefully balanced the soup bowl and opened the door, carrying the covered bowl into the kitchen and laying it on a tray with some bread and butter and a glass of water.

"Where are you, Irene?" she called. Her partner's crossword book was lying on the floor next to her fireside chair, a pen beside it, but the woman was nowhere to be seen.

"Must be in the loo," thought Rose, when there was no answer. "Back with your main course soon, "she called, before retracing her steps and going back outside into the chilly spring air. The wind had risen and was blowing hard, and the thick, dark rain clouds were beginning to form in the distant sky, building and deepening as they travelled down from the glens.

Back in the barn, Elaine too rose from the table. "Don't shut the door, please, Archie, I'm going to nip home too for a moment," she said, wrapping her jacket loosely round her shoulders. "I forgot to bring over the cream to go with pudding. I'll whip it over there, so don't wait for me to start your next course!"

She left quickly, and Archie carefully closed the heavy barn door, dropping the latch to make sure it didn't swing open and let the heat out. The soup was finished and there was some chat while the company let the first course digest.

"I wonder what's keeping Sam?" Jo asked. "Should we keep the soup warm, do you think?"
"Och, we can soon heat up a bowl for her in the microwave," said Maureen, laying her hand on Jo's arm. "Just relax!" she smiled.

Jennifer and Frankie exchanged a quick glance and Frankie suppressed a smile. It was nice to see these women so loved up, she thought. Really nice.
"Tell you what, I'll go over to Ploughman's Rest in a minute and check how the food's doing, and put the plates into warm," suggested Jennifer. "I'll knock on Sam's door when I've done that, and see how her quiches are coming along!" The barn door was opened once again a few minutes later, as Jennifer slipped out.

A few minutes later, Frankie looked round at the others. "Jen's taking her time, I'll go over and help her," she said. "I don't know what's keeping everyone else!"

As she walked to the door, it suddenly swung open. Rose and Elaine stood there, Elaine carrying a large bowl of whipped cream.

"We've been setting the recycling bins upright," said Rose. "We were both almost here when we heard a crash coming from the car park, that wind is really getting up now!"

"That's the worst of it when they've just been emptied," said Elaine. "Doesn't take much to blow them over. Maybe we should ask the council for big metal bins like they have for flats?"

The women took their places and the conversation became heated as the pros and cons of a larger bin were discussed.

Maureen was explaining about the collection system for the Edinburgh tenements when the door opened slowly and Frankie entered.

Her face was blanched paper white and her eyes were round and huge, with fear in them.

"What's wrong?" Jo was the first to speak.

"It's, it's Sam," she said. "Jennifer has just found her on the floor in Ploughman's. I, I think… I think she's dead."

There was so little blood, it seemed impossible that she had died. The quarry tiled kitchen floor near her head had a smear of sticky, drying blood. Sam lay, looking as peaceful as if she was merely sleeping, and even in death, her beauty was undeniable and striking.

That stunning face, which had broken so many hearts, was blanched and still; the wide blue eyes stared upwards, unseeing; her long, shapely legs splayed, slumped and inert. Her arms were crooked at odd angles, as if she'd tried to break her fall.

The women stood at the kitchen door, gazing in horror, a strange inertia freezing them into immobility as they took in the scene: the body, the signs of a scuffle, a broken plate and overturned chairs.

Maureen's nursing instinct overrode her revulsion at the scene, and she checked for signs of life, without disturbing the position of the body. "I'm afraid she's dead," she said, rising to her feet and rejoining the others at the doorway.

Jennifer broke the silence in a voice fractured with fear and bewilderment. "I'll call the police. We should leave everything as it is till they get here." In silence, they moved out of the cottage and Jennifer secured the door with the master set of keys.

In the farmhouse courtyard, a bitter spring wind lashed the huddled group of women, who stood with Archie, stunned into a bleak silence.

The stones of the old buildings groaned faintly in the wind. They'd known, felt the sinister stirrings, the malign feelings growing over the months until their ancient frames shuddered. Now it had happened, and she lay dead, her blood leaching into their fabric, their history. The wind gathered pace and flung sharp sleet around the courtyard as night loomed down.

Chapter 21
The Police Investigation Begins

"Dead, alright," said the duty medical examiner, rising to her feet and removing the latex gloves. "We'll have to do a proper examination, but it looks like she hit her temple on the quarry tiles and that's what's caused the fatal brain bleed. Looks like there's some bruising to her arms and face as well," she added.

"Thanks, Pam." DI Emma Ferguson nodded to the doctor, looked carefully around the room, noting the signs of struggle. "Fire me over the forensics report as soon as, please." "Will do," said Pam Kelly, stepping out of her white coveralls and picking up her bag. "Good luck with this one, Emma!"

The police photographer continued his work, while DI Ferguson spoke to her colleague. "I want the cottage sealed off, and also the one next door where this woman lived, and I want them kept that way until the fingerprinting and other forensic examinations are completed.

"The owner of the farmhouse, Jennifer Armstrong, has suggested we use her study to interview each of the women, oh, and the one man, as a preliminary step. Put an officer into the barn with them meantime and I'll talk with them one at a time."

"Ok, boss," said DS Brian Crawford, heading for the door and calling for a couple of his team.

Soon afterwards, a crew went into Ploughman's Rest, emerging with the shrouded figure on the trolley and loading it into the back of the waiting ambulance.

The wind whipped fiercely round the buildings, and the old timbers moaned faintly. A distant crash signalled that the recycling bin had been blown over again.

Inside the barn, Archie and the women huddled on the benches, as the unwanted food congealed and grew cold on the trestle table.

One by one, they were called to Jennifer's study, where they were questioned by DI Ferguson as to their movements that day: where had they been and when, had any strangers been noticed in the area recently, did Sam have any enemies?"

"That's all for now," said DI Ferguson, entering the barn after the last person had been questioned. "You're all free to return home now, but please stay locally for the next few days. We'll be talking to you all again in more detail soon, at Forfar Police Station. We'll have the post mortem report soon, but in view of the signs of struggle, we're treating this as a suspicious death."

Numbed, silent and fearful, the women returned to their homes, but had no wish to be alone. Jennifer spent the night at Frankie's, Jo stayed at Maureen's, Elaine and Archie sat up in her cottage till the wind finally dropped and a weak dawn filtered into the sky. They then went wearily to bed, holding each other tightly until at last fatigue overwhelmed them and they fell into troubled sleep.

Rose and Irene slumped in chairs before the fire, an uneasy silence broken only by Irene coughing from time to time. "I'll sleep in the spare room," said Irene, eventually. "Let you get some sleep, Rose." She rose and headed for the stairs, and Rose thought, inconsequentially, how much older Irene looked, all of a sudden.

The residents of Barleyknowe lay in their beds, troubled and sad. But not all had an extra fear in their head that night.

The fear of being found out.

Chapter 22
Red Herrings

The days which followed the ghastly discovery of Sam's body took on a surreal quality as the Barleyknowe residents tried their best to come to terms with the death. Jennifer, as unofficial leader of the community, had the hardest time. "Bloody journalists! Why won't they leave us alone?" she asked Frankie in exasperation one night, as she slammed the phone down on a tabloid reporter, wanting to know the background details of the dead woman.

"It's the nature of the set-up here, Jen," Frankie said, switching on the kettle for the umpteenth time that morning. Tea stocks were running low with the constant ebb and flow of visitors: the other women, their family members and the police.

"It's unusual to have an all-woman community just like this one: it's no wonder that there's interest from the media."

"I wish they'd all just leave us alone! This whole situation is like a waking nightmare." The normally calm Jen ran her hands through her hair in a gesture of frustration and fear. "If only we knew how it happened, who did this awful thing…"

Frankie handed her a mug of tea and shivered. "That's the worst bit, isn't it? Wondering who would do such a thing, and why? If it had been an accident, the person would surely have rushed to get help, and they didn't, so it leaves us with the conclusion it wasn't an accident! Or did someone panic and bolt?

" Did you notice any strangers around recently? Can't say I did, we get so few people here that one of us would have noticed, there's enough of us at home all the time to spot a stranger or visitor immediately! We even notice and comment when we have a different postie! Or was it someone sleeping rough in the other barn, and it was a robbery gone wrong…" She tailed off, a worried look on her face.

Jen shook her head slowly. "I just can't work it out. The police seem to think, from the forensic and other evidence, that it might have been an argument which got out of hand and ended violently, and they seem to have ruled out a random stranger being involved: no sight or sound of anyone being around here, no strange cars, and no motive either, so maybe we should just forget about that theory.

"The fingerprints haven't helped to eliminate any of us, because we were all in and out of the cottage that day, and in the days beforehand, and all our prints are everywhere. Archie's the only one whose prints don't feature, except on a casserole dish which Elaine brought over..." She looked fearfully at Frankie. "What if the person is planning another attack, and will do it before the police find out who did it?"

Frankie sat down and put her arms around her. "Shhhh, darling. The police are doing their best, and being very thorough. There's still two officers posted outside Ploughman's Rest, we're safe!"

Holding Jennifer close, she said: "I don't know how many times they expect us to tell them where we were and for how long that day. It's hard to remember exactly and I don't want to trip up! I'm sick of going over it all with the police down at the station, it doesn't matter how they ask it, it's always the same answers I give, because I'm only telling them the little I know. And all this stuff they ask about Sam, was she liked, did she have friends here, had she fallen out with anyone?"

Suddenly, she sat upright. "Jen, did you tell her about... the kiss Sam and I had? I mentioned it when the DI asked if I was close to her, and I had to say something..."

Jen looked at her. "Yes, I told her, Frankie. It gives me reason to be angry with her, to dislike her, but hardly enough to kill her! Besides which, I've an alibi: I was with everyone else in the barn."

The colour drained from Frankie's face. "But, Jen, you left us to go and check the food, and you said you'd find out how Sam was getting on with her quiches... then I came over and found you there, just stock still, staring at Sam's body...Oh god, surely they won't suspect you?"

***

In the incident room at the local police station, DI Ferguson and her Detective Sergeant sat on opposite sides of a large desk, piled high with papers and discarded coffee cups.

"Right, Brian," said Emma Ferguson, handing him a fresh mug of tea. "Let's take a step back and consider what we know about the death of Sam Taylor. I'm leaning towards a scuffle or fight, hence the bruising the pathologist noted, which escalated into a shove or push, and the woman fell, striking her head in just the wrong way, on a hard surface.

"So my guts are telling me this is not a planned murder. However, whoever did this left the woman to die. We'll never know if she could have been saved if help had been called... that smacks of someone having no inclination to save Sam Taylor's life."

She paused. "However, there seems to be more suspects and more motives than we usually have, wouldn't you say? This woman seems to have been a first class trouble-maker, and ruffled quite a few feathers!"

Her colleague laughed shortly. "I'll say! Sam's been what my sister calls a player: somebody who knows they're attractive and just takes who and when and what she wants, regardless! That woman Irene was obviously besotted with her, and I think Frankie had a soft spot too...snogging in the barn and all that. You couldn't make half of this lot up, boss!"

The DI looked down at her notepad. "I agree about Irene, and Frankie for that matter, and we have to remember they also each have partners who would be less than happy to hear about infidelities. Taking a pen, she began jotting down some bullet points.

"Rose, Irene, Jennifer and Elaine all had opportunity to do this, as they were all out of the barn with no witnesses for short periods that afternoon. Irene was housebound with a sore throat, but when Rose took her over soup, she wasn't in the sitting room and didn't respond to her call. Mind you, we've only Rose's word for that, and they've both got strong motive for quarrelling with Sam. Irene's admitted the affair and its abrupt ending only a few days ago, and Rose has told us about the note she found under the spare bed.

"These are two very angry and sad women, and in Irene's case, she's a woman who's been used and abused then dumped. Nothing as terrible as a woman spurned, young Brian, and don't you forget that!"

"Sure thing, boss," he said, grinning. "Not that I'm in a hurry to spurn my lovely Maria, she's amazing!"

"I know," said Emma, "but just you remember that she's a civil engineer and has access to sharp instruments if you don't behave yourself!"

Turning back to her notes, she continued: "Elaine Turner told us that Sam had spilled the beans to Archie's wife Jean, causing her to fling Archie out. Mind you, he had that coming from all accounts, he hasn't exactly been Mr Faithful.

" However, that does mean Elaine had cause to be very angry with Sam. To the point of murder is debatable, of course, but I still think this was accidental.

" She had opportunity too, going back home to prepare cream for the dessert. She's admitted freely that she did the small acts of vandalism at Sam's, the disappeared washing and emptied flower pots, but that doesn't point to murder. I suspect those little acts were enough for her to get her own back.

"Jennifer found the body, but she too was away from everyone for enough time to quarrel with Sam. She certainly has a reason to be very hacked off with her."

Brian refilled the kettle. "There's a terrible intensity, almost an incestuous hot-house effect with all these women out there in the middle of nowhere, with passions and jealousies running high. It's like something out of a Tennessee Williams play with a strong Sapphic element!"

DI Ferguson dropped her pen and laughed so loudly Brian almost dropped the coffee jar. "You crack me up, Brian," she chuckled. "I'm never allowed to forget that you did English literature and psychology at Uni! I must say, you always bring a well-honed phrase or two to our investigations. What was it you said to me about those two young neds we found had been thieving clothes from washing lines in Arbroath then tried to sell them at a car boot sale…in Arbroath!"

Brian smiled: "I think what I said that day was: 'if they'd a brain cell between them they'd be dangerous,' nothing very literary!" He set down the mugs of coffee and they began again.

Emma Ferguson looked seriously across at her young colleague. "I know there's an unusual element to this case, but at the end of the day, a young woman has lost her life and someone is responsible. She had plenty of people who disliked her, and not just at Barleyknowe. Sam Taylor seems to have cause havoc, trouble and distress wherever she went. Sounds like a complex and troubled woman, why and how we'll never know for sure, as there doesn't seem to be much in the way of relatives.

"All we've managed to trace is this cousin, Imogen, who lives in Paris. She's on her way over here to arrange the funeral and see to the business side of things. Sam left a Will, her solicitor has confirmed, leaving her flat to this woman Ali, an ex, we think, and a shed load of cash to her old art school, the PDSA and a charity which helps kids being bullied at school or on social media. Maybe she had a heart underneath it all?

"So, getting back to the case, we have motive of sorts from Elaine, Rose, Irene, Jennifer, Archie and Frankie. Archie has a solid alibi for the time we know the death occurred, so we're left with the other five.

" I think Frankie was only out of sight for such a short time before she returned to the barn with Jennifer, less than a minute, and the timing of the death was earlier, so I think we can rule her out. Her motivation is weak, in any case.

She paused. "So we're down to Elaine, Rose, Irene and Jennifer. Any instinctive gut feelings here?"

Brian doodled on the pad before him. "I agree with you that I think it's been an accidental death, and also that all of these four are in the frame, but the key point, as you've said, is that Sam was left to die. That changes everything.

He looked across at his boss. "I don't think it was Elaine and I also don't think it was Jennifer Armstrong. According to her story, and to Frankie's, they made it up after Frankie confessed to the stolen kiss with Sam in the barn, and she knew Sam was leaving Barleyknowe soon anyway. The timing doesn't quite fit: she wasn't away from the others long enough to fight with Sam before Frankie arrived and found her staring at the body."

"They could be in cahoots, though," said his DI. "Frankie would want to protect her girlfriend, wouldn't she?"

Brian chewed the end of his pencil. "I think it's either Rose or Irene."

The two detectives looked at each other for a long few moments.

"Right," said DI Ferguson. "Let's get them both in here again for questioning as murder suspects. Tell them either to get a lawyer or we'll appoint duty solicitors to act for them, as we'll be bringing charges. Bring them in separate cars and keep them well apart here at the station. We don't want any collusion."

Irene and Rose arrived at the police station, getting out of the cars almost simultaneously. They glanced at each other across the rain-streaked car park, but no words were spoken as they followed the police officers indoors to separate interview rooms where their lawyers sat, flicking through binders of notes. "This could be a long haul," DI Ferguson said to her colleague. "They've already both claimed complete ignorance of the death and have played down their animosity towards Sam Taylor. Our evidence is circumstantial and fairly weak right now, we'll just need to see how it goes."

Brian Crawford looked at her thoughtfully. "Maybe you're right, boss, but I've an odd feeling about this one, just an instinct..."

"Well, let's hope you're right and we get this out of the way as soon as possible, with the right result of course," Emma Ferguson replied.

Two hours later, the detectives sat in the canteen, staring at each other in disbelief.

"That ended not with a bang, but a whimper, in the words of TS Eliot!" said Brian. "You owe me a fish supper. Telt you I had a feeling about this one!"

"I've just never seen that happen before, never!" said Emma Ferguson, shaking her head in disbelief. "Both come in here, having previously been adamant that they had nothing to do with it, then they both change their stories and say they did it!

"Did you see their briefs' faces? That young lawyer from the Arbroath office turned almost green when Rose said she'd shoved Sam, not meaning to do her any real harm, but just panicked when she saw her hit the deck and couldn't rouse her?"

Brian smiled wryly. "Then half an hour later in the next room, it's Irene saying she hit Sam and grabbed her arms, that's why there was the bruising. I think that despite everything, those two are trying to protect each other by taking the blame."

"Let's just take a step back and see what we've now got," said the DI. "There's a general consensus in the two stories, but enough difference to make it plausible, wouldn't you say?

"The women went independently, and unknown to the other, to Ploughman's Rest to confront Sam. They both knew Sam was using the oven there before joining the others in the barn. Irene went there first, slipping out of her house soon after Rose left for the barn.

"She says she wanted answers as to why Sam had dumped her, and it escalated into a physical fight when the crockery was smashed and chairs overturned. Irene says she was devastated at the rejection and fearful that Rose would find out about the affair. She admits to having a bad temper and says it just got the better of her, in the face of Sam's indifference and nasty comments."

Brian Crawford took over, looking at his yellow pad of notes. "So, the noise of the fight is muffled by the high winds and the solid doors on the properties. That figures. Rose arrives to find the rammy in full spate, and tells them both she knows about the affair. Irene begs her forgiveness, and it could have ended at that point."

"Yes, but Sam couldn't resist a few digs, could she?" said the DI. "She taunted Rose with explicit details of her and Irene in the bedroom, and that's where things went pear-shaped. Rose admits to pushing her, hard, as Sam tried to get past her and out of the door, and we know the rest. They've both admitted leaving Sam unconscious on the floor, and failing to get medical attention for her. I keep coming back to it, Brian, a young woman is dead. It's murder.

"I'll call the Fiscal and say we've enough to charge them both with murder," she added. "We'll keep them both in custody overnight for appearance at the High Court in the morning."

She rose to her feet, and passed a weary hand across her brow. "There's something sad about this case, Brian. These are two essentially decent women, who've just been used and played by Sam Taylor. Their lives will never be the same again."

She stopped, watching the expression on her colleague's face. "Before you say anything, of course it's all wrong that a woman died, I'm not going soft in my old age, believe me! Right, just let me do the calls and paperwork and that fish supper awaits you. I'll nip along to the chippie…pickled onions too?"

***

Six months later

"Oh my god," said Frankie, reading The Scotsman from her chair by the fire in Jennifer's house. "Rose's lawyer called this an accident, not a *crime passionel* and says there were so many mitigating circumstances that his client should go free immediately!

Jen looked up from her iPad. "The judge thought differently, though, didn't he? They accepted a lesser plea from Rose of culpable homicide, so it's a four year jail sentence for her, then out on licence.
"We'll never know if Sam's life could have been saved if either of them had acted quickly instead of fleeing in a panic, apparently rushing back to their house for a hurried conversation, to decide what to do.

"From the medical examiner's report, it does sound as if Sam died almost instantly, so perhaps her life couldn't have been saved regardless of the few minutes delay before she was found by Jennifer. Rose might have had a longer sentence if she hadn't admitted it, though, and I guess she'll be out in a couple of years with good behaviour."

She scrolled down. "Irene's got off lightly, if you ask me, on her charges of assault. 200 hours community service, but even that would have been less if there hadn't been the previous assault conviction on her record. I wonder what that was all about?She did always strike me as a woman suppressing a deep anger, so it doesn't come as a complete surprise. I suspected there was a drink issue there too, there were an awful lot of empties in their recycling box!"

"The tabloids are all over this one," said Frankie, dropping the paper and thumbing through her 'phone." 'Lesbian love triangle ends in death' 'Teachers sentenced for death of lover' 'Death in rural commune.'" She shifted in her seat. The two women stared at each other for a long minute.

Eventually, Jennifer spoke, in a quiet, sad voice. "I'll need to think what's best to do, and not make any decisions yet, Frankie. Let the dust settle first."

***

Across the country, in Bearsden, Freya was also reading the morning paper. She's gone out early to buy The Guardian ..."so balanced, dear," she'd once told her long-suffering cleaning lady Linda one morning, "and I adore the culture sections!"

Linda made a non-committal reply and began waxing the dining room table.

She had a soft spot for Freya and didn't mind a bit of eccentricity, heaven knows she had plenty of that amongst her clients, but Freya's hypocrisy and patronising manner was at times hard to take.

"She sees me as a lower being, not a person of worth," she thought, rubbing in the polish with vigour. "One of these days, probably the moment when I hand in my notice, I might tell her that I have a degree in mathematical physics but as a single parent I have to take what I can get, including bolt-on jobs like cleaning to make ends meet."

She paused to retrieve a duster which had fallen to the floor. "On the other hand, maybe not! Maybe I shouldn't tell her. It would just buy into her snobbery and preconceptions and she'd instantly treat me differently, I'd be 'one of them'," she mused.

"Lucky I know who I am and my worth, whether I'm scrubbing toilets or doing complex maths, I'm the same person!"

Freya's trip to the newsagents that morning didn't just result in a pint of milk and the Guardian in her shopping basket. The Daily Record had a front page splash with the heading: "Angus love and death tangle: two sentenced."

The red top was slipped into her basket under the Guardian, and she asked the assistant for a carrier bag. It was worth the extra 5p to hide her purchase.

Later that day, Freya was holding court to an interested circle of friends. She's gathered them round to her house, with great excitement and, having poured herbal tea, she waved the tabloid at them. "I just had to buy this today when I saw the front page!" she gushed. "That's where I went on my retreat, you now, to write my epic poem, the very cottage where Sam Taylor lived after me! To think, I could have been caught up in all that! I knew there were things going on!"

"Well, you weren't there at the time Sam Taylor was, and you weren't having an affair with the teacher," said one of her friends, wryly. She was used to Freya's melodramas, but in fairness, she had lived in this community for a time and got to know the women.

"Of course I didn't have an affair with Irene," said Freya, sharply, "but I knew there were undercurrents, a seething black morass underneath that politeness. I'm never wrong, I know people... are you alright, dear?" she asked as one of the circle stifled a laugh, turning it into a cough.

Chapter 23
The Community Falls Apart

The women, plus Archie, assembled in the barn, once again seated at the trestle table. This time, though, the long wooden table wasn't laid with food and drink, or cheerful crockery. Notepads were laid out, and there was no banter and laughter amongst those seated there. Their solemn faces reflected the gravity of the meeting.

Jennifer sat down calmly, her iPad and notebook ready. A tiny thought flickered in her head. "By god, you're good, Jennifer! That business head switch works every time for you, however dire the situation!" Looking round, she began, her voice calm and cool. "Thanks for coming along today, it makes it easier with everyone being here except for Rose and Irene. We know where they are and why. I understand that Irene's planning to help with an adult literacy programme as part of her community service, if anyone is interested."

A faint murmur went round the table, but no-one spoke out loud.

"Anyhow, we all know what's happened and I'm aware there is a feeling amongst some of you that you don't want to stay here any longer. We'll go round the table in a moment, but just to let you know at the outset, Irene has contacted me through her solicitor to say that they want to sell up here and move away. Whether that's together or separately is their business," she said, quelling the murmurs round the table.

"Let's just focus on the practicalities as much as we can, and leave the emotions to one side."

Elaine cleared her throat. "I'd like to tell you my thoughts," she said, looking round the table. "Archie and I plan to stay together, wherever that will be in the future. This decision has been not exactly forced on us, there are other options, but let's just say, Sam telling his wife about our relationship and them finally parting for good, has brought the situation to a head for us.

"Cards on the table, I'm planning to sell my hairdressing businesses and would also like to sell Springburn. Archie and his wife intend to divorce and once the finances are settled, we'll buy a place together. We're not sure where we'll be going as yet."

"Thanks, Elaine," said Jennifer, making a note on her yellow pad.

Jo spoke next. "Maureen and I," she hesitated, smiling at the woman next to her, "...well, we plan to marry and..." she broke off as there were murmurs of congratulation from the others. " We've decided after much thought, that we don't want to stay here." Maureen broke in. "There are happy memories of our time here, of course, and we wouldn't have met otherwise, but after what's happened, well, we'd rather have a fresh start somewhere else. So, we're planning to sell Dairy Cottage and Marchmont."

"This makes it easier than I feared," said Jennifer. "The plain truth is that I've no appetite to stay here either. Frankie and I will probably move to Edinburgh, our plans aren't fixed yet, but as I own the farmhouse and the ...the other cottages... it might be better and easier to sell the complex as a whole. You will, of course, each receive the sale price for your individual properties."

She looked round the table. "I'm very sad that this hasn't worked out as I hoped it would do: I had a dream of happy living up here, but sadly, it's been spoiled beyond repair. You're all lovely people and I'll be sorry to part company with you, but it's very understandable that you all want away from being faced with the memory of what happened on a daily basis. It's been very traumatic for all of us.

"Would you trust me to try and sell Barleyknowe as a whole? I've a number of contacts in the property world and will do my utmost to ensure we all come out of this no worse than we began."

There were nods of agreement round the table, and Jennifer flipped her writing pad closed. "Leave it with me, and I'll let you know how I get on."

The stones, the timbers of the cottages listened and heard, then settled quietly to wait. They'd waited so many times before and would wait again. Whoever was going to be next, would come along in time. Meantime, they'd wait, and watch and listen.

Chapter 24
New Lives

"I hadn't realised how much I'd missed being able to get to the Filmhouse," smiled Maureen, sipping a glass of Shiraz and glancing around the café bar. "The nachos are lovely here, Jo, want to share some with me?" Jo smiled back at her, and rose to go to the counter. "It's getting busy, I'll go over now and order so we've time to enjoy lunch before the film."

"Och, it's always like this a festival time," said Maureen. "What a great buzz there is around! Oh, there's somebody I know from when I lived Marchmont: Alison who went to yoga classes with me! Hang on, I'll bring her over!"

Jo smiled again. Maureen had blossomed since they got together. It was as if her emotional baggage, her burden of guilt, shame and regret, had been if not discarded, at least put away somewhere, lessened.

They'd exchanged their stories, their guilty feelings and past mistakes over the course of one long night, and somehow getting their stories out into the air reduced their potency and power to hurt and trouble.

"I'll never forget how badly I treated Wendy," Jo said, as they watched the fire roar up the chimney of Dairy Cottage. "That was one of the worst mistakes I ever made, one of the worst things I ever did in my life. I behaved shockingly towards a lovely woman."

Maureen took her hand. "She knew that you loved her, Jo. She knew that for sure, and she forgave you, being the sweet and kind person you've described to me. Jo, nobody's perfect, not one single person that's ever walked the earth.

"We all make mistakes, errors of judgement, we say the wrong things and fail to say the right ones, we're all carried away at times by emotions and circumstances. It's the human condition to be flawed and at times, very foolish.

"I regret so much having an affair with a married man, a man that I knew perfectly well had a wife and children, and then facing the horror of having to abort the baby, which meant I couldn't go back to the church. It was a sin, and I knew it. As for helping him falsify the records after the woman died…I still think about her, and her poor family, and the terrible thing I did colluding with him like that."

Jo looked at her. "You were very young, Maureen, young and impressionable. The man was to blame, he treated you shabbily and he'll have had to live with that knowledge ever since. You've spent a working lifetime helping and caring for people, saving them. If there is a god, I'm sure you've made recompense for the early errors in your life."

Maureen threw another log on the fire.

"Well, I think we're both not exactly off the moral hook, Jo, but perhaps it's time we began to forgive ourselves and stopped beating ourselves up."

They'd married, quietly and without fuss, in a registry office in Dundee, shortly before moving to Edinburgh. Their terraced house in the city's Shandon area was Edwardian, but had been modernised and had a small garden front and back.

"Perfect!" said Maureen when they first viewed it. "So handy for everything, yet in a quiet street!"

Looking round the house, and gazing from the sitting room window towards the street, Maureen had a sudden lurch of happiness, one of those moments when you just know you're contented and excited at the same time.

"Edinburgh, I've missed you so much!" she thought, watching the red buses trundle along the busy street. "I'm home, and home with the person I love!"

She'd been right, thought Jo, unpacking some boxes in their new home a couple of months later. The house was in a quiet street, but only minutes by bus into the centre of Edinburgh. She slit open another carton and began emptying books onto shelves, pausing as she lifted out Wendy's poetry books. "I hope, wherever you are, my dear, you've forgiven me, and you're happy for me," she thought, tears clouding her eyes. She heard Maureen singing as she clattered around in the nearby kitchen. "I've got a second shot at happiness, and this time, I'm not going to mess it up this time, Wendy."

She placed the poetry books carefully on the shelf and glanced out of the window. A dreich Edinburgh morning, where small rain had fallen among the tangled flowers in their garden, had given way to watery sunshine. She continued to stare out of the window, one of Wendy's poetry books still in her hand. Then, raising her gaze, she saw in the clearing sky, arching splendid, colourful and wonderful, a huge, hopeful, redeeming and forgiving rainbow…

Jo turned her attention back to the present, and the friendly bustle of the Filmhouse, and was introduced to Maureen's friend Alison.

"It's great to have you back in town," the woman said. "Hope you'll both come round for dinner one night." Maureen beamed at the woman. "We'd love that, thank you!"

We. That special word that she'd missed for so long. We. She was with someone she loved and who loved her too. She read somewhere that love looks for someone to land upon, but she hadn't been looking for love, it had just happened, completely out of the blue, an unexpected and blissfully wonderful stroke of luck in meeting Jo. She had someone to share life's ups and downs with, a companion and a confidante. It had taken a whole, sad lifetime but she could now honestly say it.

She was happy, and there was another reason for her contentment besides being back home and with the person she loved. One day, when Jo was busy putting up shelves in their new home, she went out to locate the nearest corner shop, post office and chemist, reveling in their new neighbourhood.

At the end of a run of pleasant sandstone villas, she came upon a church with its doors open wide. The priest could be seen in the church porch taking down a poster advertising a bring and buy sale. On impulse, Maureen walked briskly along the gravel path and into the church, where she first genuflected, then took a seat in a pew. How much she'd missed the comfort of the church! All these years, consumed by guilt and shame about her affair, and the abortion…

"How are you today? It looks like the rain's staying off at least." The priest was standing in the aisle, smiling at her through thick-lensed spectacles. "I haven't seen you here before, are you new to the area?"

"My, my wife Jo and I have just moved here," Maureen began, hesitancy in her voice. The priest smiled warmly at her. "Welcome!" he said. "I hope you'll both enjoy living here. It's a grand area, and the neighbours are friendly! It's a myth about us Edinburgh folk being standoffish! I'm Father O'Connor, by the way."

He didn't flinch there, Maureen noted. Not a flicker of disapproval about same-sex marriage. She took his outstretched hand and shook it warmly.

"Would you like a cup of tea?" Father O'Connor motioned to the Vestry. "I've even got some home baking left over from the bring and buy sale on Saturday."

It was like a dam bursting. Maureen sat with the priest, her teacup shaking as she wept, recovered herself and wept again, the tears riveting down her face, as she told him the sad, ancient story about her affair with the married doctor and the termination.

Father O'Connor listened patiently, letting the decades of pent-up guilt flow from the woman before him.

At last, as Maureen stopped crying, the priest gently took her hand. "My dear, you've carried a heavy burden and suffered for so long. You must forgive the man involved and in turn, you must seek forgiveness from God. You'll do penance, and we'll talk later about how best that can be done, but please begin to forgive yourself too."

Outside in the fresh air, Maureen looked to the sky, grey and soft with cloud and strewn with ticks of black birds wheeling in the autumn breeze. Then, with purpose, she turned the corner towards her home, and towards the future.

***

It had to happen. It was entirely inevitable, that Frankie would bump into Marion, now she and Jennifer were back living in Edinburgh.

"Does this suit me?" Frankie picked up a turquoise fascinator from the stand and, fixing it to her curls, turned towards Jennifer. "What do you think? I reckon this colour's a good match for my dress, or is it too blue?" She turned her head in the mirror, adjusting the headpiece slightly. "I'd have dragged Johnny along today to help us choose but it's maybe unlucky for him to see what his best maid is wearing!"

"It's not so bad for you! I'm combining mother of one of the grooms with giving him away, that's even worse. What a responsibility they've given us!" chuckled Jen, trying on a wide brimmed, coral hat. "What do you think? Is this overpowering?"

Turning her head from side to side in front of the mirror, she asked: "Or maybe I should ask Ross: a fashion photographer should know what looks good! Would it be unlucky for him to see what his new mother-in-law intends to wear?"

Biting her lip, she suddenly looked serious. "It's just such a shame Johnny's mum isn't well enough to be there, to see him married to such a nice guy. Did you know they plan to go up afterwards to the nursing home? Sounds like she mostly doesn't know who he is now, but maybe it'll be one of her better days, I hope so…"

She broke off and turned round.

Frankie didn't answer. She was staring across John Lewis hat section, towards the escalator, and all the colour had left her face. Browsing amongst the handbags, a preoccupied expression on her face, was Marion.

For a moment, Frankie felt that familiar sick, emptiness in her stomach, the sensation of loss, yearning, sadness, jealousy and anguish all rolled into one horrible feeling. She actually felt as if she was going to be sick, right there on the spot, amid the sophisticated elegance of the hat section.

"What's wrong?" said Jennifer, holding her arm, concern in her eyes. "You look like you've seen a ghost!"

Frankie drew in a deep breath and whispered: "That's Marion over there, next to the handbags. She's… she's got her girls with her!" Two small children could now be seen joining their mother, the younger one tugging at her coat and pointing in the direction of the toy department. "Go and speak to her, Frankie," urged Jennifer." You should. I'll wait here."

"No! Please, come with me," said Frankie, moving purposefully towards the handbags. "Hello, Marion," she said quietly, touching the woman's sleeve.

Marion looked at her blankly for a split second, then Jennifer watched as realisation dawned and a series of emotions travelled across Marion's face. Tears began to fill her eyes, but she quickly pulled herself together. The two small girls watched their mother attentively, unsure what was happening.

"Frankie!" Marion exclaimed. "How good to see you again! Girls, this is mummy's friend Frankie who used to be in my book group."

"God, she's good," Jennifer thought. "Amazing what in-built manners do for you in these situations!"

Frankie too had recovered her composure. "This is Jennifer, "she said, simply. Marion stretched out her hand and shook Jennifer's: a light, warm touch.

"Are you still living up in Angus?" asked Marion. "I'd heard through the book group that you'd moved up north and wondered if that recent court case was anywhere near you..." she tailed off. "Yes, it was where we both lived," Frankie said, holding Marion's gaze and fighting for control of her voice. "The whole development was sold after the... incident...most of us wanted a clean break from the place. Jennifer and I are in Edinburgh now, living up in Bruntsfield, handy for everything and near to the great coffee shops!" she added.

Marion gave a weak smile. "Well, it's nice you're back here again, Frankie, I never really saw you as a country dweller." There was the faintest tremor in her voice, almost indiscernible. "I hope you'll be happy now you're back here."

Frankie chatted a little to the girls then said: "What are you up to these days, Marion?"

"Much the same old usual," she said. "Yoga, book club, seeing friends, all quite mundane, really. There is some news though, we're moving to East Lothian. Alistair's landed a deputy head's post and it's just too far for him to commute every day from Edinburgh. We're hoping to be settled over the summer holidays – we have a new house and ours is sold. We want to be all sorted for the girls starting school in August and before the new baby arrives…" She tailed off, and for the first time, Frankie noticed the bump, which had been hidden by her loose coat. "We're hoping that the baby is a boy this time, aren't we girls?"

The two children nodded in unison. "We went to the hospital with mummy last time and the lady doing the scan said it's a boy", said the older girl.

"That'll be nice for you," said Jennifer, covering Frankie's silence. "I'm sure these two will be a big help with the baby!"

"We must be going," said Marion. "Alistair is meeting us soon and we're going upstairs to look at furniture. The new house is a bit bigger and needs some extra bits and pieces," said Marion, brightly. "It's been nice to see you, Frankie," she said, giving her the briefest hug. "And good to meet you, Jennifer. I hope you'll enjoy city life!"

Taking each of the girls by the hand, she turned towards the escalator, and once on it, looked across to where Jennifer and Frankie stood.

The air seemed to solidify, turn thick and oppressive, and the chatter and movement faded and halted. All that moved was a crackling, lightning bolt burning, flaring, searing between them, as Marion and Frankie connected, intensely, for what they both knew was a final time, a closing and a drawing of the line under what had been their huge and fatally flawed love. Marion felt a shift on the axis of her life and within, her baby moved uneasily, the adrenalin surge washing through the womb.

The kaleidoscope of emotions, memories, laughter, anguish and tears settled into a single sentence and the words in her head reached Frankie, fizzing and racing from one heart to the other.

"I'll always love you. I'm so very sorry that I hurt you."

***

In Perth, Elaine paused from unpacking a large tea chest filled with china.

"Let's call it a day, Archie," she said. "We're both done in. The rest of this can wait till tomorrow, or even till next week! I'll stick the kettle on."

Archie rose to his feet from his position on the kitchen floor where he'd been unwrapping pots and pans. Holding the table edge for support, and staggering a little, he stood upright and nodded. "Good idea! It's an Indian takeaway and an early night for us. We've all the time in the world to sort the house out." Elaine smiled at him and filled the kettle, picking out two mugs from a pile of unmatched cups on the kitchen table.

"I hope we've made the right choice and will be happy here, Archie," she called through to him. "I must say, I'm looking forward to having a garden and some outside space, it'll be lovely to sit out in the summer months."

"Yes," agreed Archie, as he walked through to the sitting room and sat down heavily on the sofa. "Never thought of myself as a bungalow man, to be truthful, but it makes sense not to have stairs to think about as we get older. And maybe having a garden to see to will get rid of some of this excess poundage I seemed to have developed in the last few months. The down side of being happy, eh?"

He heard Elaine chuckle as she poured their drinks. No need to worry her just now about these wee twinges he'd been having, it was probably all the stress of the divorce and moving house… he'd see about it once they got themselves registered with a new doctor. It could all wait. A few minutes later, they chinked steaming mugs of tea. "To our new home!" Elaine smiled.

"And to our new life together, where nobody knows us!" laughed Archie. "Mind you, I'm planning to get my name about on the local music scene so I can get back to some playing again: that's been seriously neglected!"

"Good idea," said Elaine, thoughtfully. "I know how much you miss that. I was thinking of picking up my scissors again too, and doing a little bit of hairdressing, filling in as holiday relief at local salons, nothing too taxing, but I do miss the banter!"

Archie smiled at her. "At that rate, before we know it, we won't have a spare moment and we should make sure we have plenty of time together, just to enjoy life, tend the garden, go places…we're getting a second chance, Elaine, and we need to grab it!"

For an answer, Elaine set down her cup and sat beside him on the sofa, putting her arms around him. "I know," she said. "I know."

***

Billy undid the black tie and stuffed it into his suit jacket pocket.

"Tea, mum? Or something a bit stronger?" he called through to Elaine, who was hanging up her coat in the hallway.

"I'll have a whisky, son, "she said, in a voice laced with thick tears. "I didn't want to have anything stronger till the wake was over and everyone gone home... his sons were so upset, weren't they? Maybe it was just the shock, when they didn't know anything was wrong with him... but I didn't know and I lived with him!

"Yes, the boys seemed genuinely distraught, considering they wanted nothing to do with him after he left Jean. You did the right thing inviting them to the funeral, and Jean too, though I understand why she didn't feel able to be there today".

Billy poured a generous measure of whisky into a glass, added a splash of water and handed it to his mother, saying: "It's been a dreadful shock to everyone, mum, especially you. I can't tell you how sad I am... just when you were starting this new life together..."

"Jean went to the funeral parlour yesterday afternoon," said Elaine, slowly. "It was only right that she had a chance to say her goodbyes to him, privately. They were together a long time, had children and grandchildren together, and despite the problems in the marriage, they had a shared history and a long connection. That had to be respected."

Billy glanced at his mother, who was sipping her drink. He flipped the top of an alcohol-free beer and, sitting down, took a gulp. His mother smiled faintly. "You could take a beer now and then, Billy. It's not likely you'd develop a drink problem just because your dad did."

"Yes, I know that," he said, a bleakness in his voice. "But I'm just not taking the chance, mum. My wife and kids are too precious to me to risk it. I've often wondered if dad had some kind of addictive personality: it wasn't just the drink, but the gambling too…"

He paused. "I was sorry the way he went, dying of liver failure which he had been told was directly down to his drinking, but there was something horribly inevitable about it. Not even 60, too."

They sat across from each other in silence, and Elaine's eye fell on the tins of paint stacked neatly in a corner of the kitchen, under a new pack of brushes.

"Archie was going to start painting in here next week," she whispered. "That was his next project, and I was going out this week for new blinds to hang once he'd finished.

"We argued a little about the colour scheme: now, what does it matter what shade of lemon we'd chosen? Why, oh why didn't he tell me he'd been having symptoms? Something might have been done, there could have been help…" she trailed off and dabbed her eyes, looking at her son.

"Maybe he thought it was simply indigestion, maybe he didn't want to worry you, or maybe he was a typical man of his generation who didn't like going to the doctor? I don't know the answer, nobody ever will know now. "

Billy shook his head slowly as he spoke. "Mum, it's been a dreadful shock for you, an awful thing to happen, but it was so quick, he wouldn't have suffered. Maybe the exertion of digging out the vegetable plot was just the final straw for his heart, but we'll never know that for sure. He's at peace."

Elaine looked at him, sadness etched on her face. "We were happy, you know. We really loved each other and we planned to marry at some point. Not to be, though."

She drained her glass and laid it down on the table with an air of finality. "Tomorrow, Billy, we'll see to all the business details and you can help me as much as you can before you need to go back home."

"Are you sure you want to live in Manchester, mum? It's quite a change for you from living up here."

She looked at him. "Son, you and your family are the most important people in my life," she answered. "I'll buy a new-build flat in the city, near enough so I can visit you all easily, but not right on top of you. Don't worry, I'll soon make a circle of friends. I'm young retired, Billy!"

He smiled faintly. "You'll stay with us once this place is sold, while we look for something suitable near to us. The children will love having Gran Scotland so close at hand!" She laid her hand on his arm. "You're a good son," she said, simply. "I don't know how or why you've turned out so well, considering everything that happened when you were young!"

"It's because you're the best mum anyone could wish for," he replied, giving her a hug.

***

Rose and Irene looked at each other across the table in the visitors' hall. There was a faint hum of conversation from the other tables in the room.

"Always good to have a table between you in these circumstances," said Irene, immediately sensing the joke fall flat between them, landing dully on the scarred wood.

Rose stared impassively at her and gave no response. Irene shifted her gaze and looked around the room.

"Busy today," she said, watching the inmates greet partners, parents and children and begin the stilted, unnatural chat imposed by the formality of the setting. Prison guards stood, impassive, unmoved as discreet tears were shed and angry words whispered.

"Hmmm. Some people visit more regularly than others. It gets busier as the weather improves and travelling gets easier."

Rose delivered the information flatly, without any real interest or feeling.

"I'm sorry I've not been more often, but what with my community service , and dealing with the move, finding a place to live, sorting out the furniture and such like…" she tailed off, aware that Rose was staring at her, coolly. Rose, the emotional, warm woman was formal, detached and icily cold.

"That's of no consequence, Irene," she began. "I believe the money for my share of Glen View has now been moved into my solicitor's keeping until I'm released, so that's a line drawn. As we already discussed, my daughter is storing my belongings and furniture meantime, so apart from one or two loose ends about our insurance policies and pension assignments, we're pretty well done.
 I've written to both agencies removing your name as a beneficiary."

"I haven't done anything about the life insurance and such like yet," said Irene, looking taken aback. "Is there any need for urgency?"

"I suggest you deal with it promptly," said Rose. "Your choice, of course, but I don't expect you'd want me to benefit from your death?"

"Couldn't we, well, try again, Rose?" Irene's bullying bluster was absent, and a conciliatory, almost wheeling tone sat uneasily in its place.

Rose looked at her again, holding her gaze quietly. "You betrayed me, Irene," she said. "It's that simple. I put up with your browbeating, your controlling behaviour and your cruel words, all because I loved you. You cheating on me with Sam was the final straw on the haystack you'd built over many years. I take responsibility for her death, although of course I didn't intend to kill her, but the situation would never have arisen but for you and what you did…"

Rose bit her lip and tears clouded her eyes for a second, but she quickly recovered.

"Once these last bits of paperwork are done, and that should be soon, I never want to see or hear from you again in my life.

"I don't want to know where or how you are, who you're with, what you're doing. I want no contact from you, no more visits here, no letters, emails or phone calls."

"But, Rose…" Irene began, her fear palpable. "You know that I've always loved you. It was always you, from when we first met in the school labs…I regret everything that happened with Sam, I've said I'm sorry so many times! I'll be lost without you…I am already lost without you…"

Rose raised her hand, palm outwards. "Forget it, Irene. There are just some things you can't forgive and my limits are reached. I wish you no harm, Irene, we did have some good times together and you were an important part of my life for a long time, but the price was too high. I almost lost my family because of you, and I've now lost my liberty and my reputation due to you. I'll always be linked to Barleyknowe and the death, now and for the rest of my life."

She paused. "It might be an idea for you to go now. Goodbye, Irene."

Slowly, Irene pushed back her chair and pulled on her jacket. "Goodbye, Rose," she said, brokenly. "I'm, I'm sorry…" She turned and walked across the hall, her court shoes clicking and echoing on the wooden floor.

Only once Rose heard the door open and close again, and Irene's retreating, echoing footsteps became fainter, did she allow herself to cry.

Chapter 25
The Stones Settle

"Good job on that one, Ryan, it was a complicated business, but you sorted the sale out very nicely."

Mr Ross flicked through a thick sheaf of papers before sliding them carefully into a box file marked Barleyknowe, Angus.

Ryan looked up from his computer. "Well, funnily enough, I did the original sale of the properties to Ms Armstrong a few years ago, before it was all done up, when I worked at the other firm."

Mr Ross chuckled. "We did a good day's work headhunting you, Ryan. I hope you're happy with your new role as a junior partner here. I always say, the sky's the limit if you've got the ability and are prepared to graft."

Ryan smiled. "I like the work and the extra responsibility you've given me, not to mention the rise and the new company car!"

He hesitated, then said: "I thought with all the… well, trouble and publicity… it might have been hard to shift the property, but the buyer has good plans for the place: Holiday lets, retreats, small business conferences, that sort of thing. He's researched the market very thoroughly, has a good business plan in place and is confident he can make a go of it. He mentioned that he'll sell off the field to a neighbouring farmer who's apparently always had his eye on it."

"Well, good work, Ryan," said his boss, leaving the room.

At Barleyknowe, the stones whispered and groaned in the night air. Dairy Cottage, Marchmont, Meadowfields and Barleyknowe Farmhouse brisked against the evening rain, their energies positive, as they thought of their occupants. Horseshoes, Glen View, Ploughman's Rest and Springburn wept, droplets leaching out and down the mortar and spilling along the gutters, for the sadness they'd seen: for the loss of hope, for the death of a sad and troubled young woman, and the end of the dream of happiness for Elaine.

They would settle, they would embrace and welcome the next occupants, their old timbers withstanding changing fortunes in a way humans with their frailties couldn't do.

Only Ploughman's Rest was to remain difficult. A succession of plumbers and joiners, sent by the new owner, failed to find the cause of the coldness in the cottage. Radiators were bled and drained, the boiler stripped down and window seals tested. In the end, draught excluders were installed in the cottage, and visitors were urged to light the log burner on arrival.

Apart from the unexplained coldness, there had been an incident when a family from Kent who were renting the cottage, had been woken in the night by one of their children screaming. When the boy was calmed down enough to speak, he said that he'd been woken by a noise and there had been a lady standing by his bed. "She was a very pretty lady, but she had blood coming out of her head and she looked so sad!"

The parents soothed the child and settled him back to sleep, assuring him there was no-one in the house except his own family, and he must have had a bad dream, but they took some time to get back to sleep. In the morning, the husband quietly showed his wife the Google search he'd made about Barleyknowe.

The family left for home the next day, telling the letting agent that a family issue meant they needed to go home early.

Epilogue

Two Years Later.

"We should really close this Barleyknowe Facebook group. I'd forgotten all about it!" Frankie turned from her laptop and pushed her reading glasses up to her forehead.

Jennifer looked up from the book she was reading and smiled. "You're so cute when you do that!"

Frankie laughed. "Yes, you've said that a few times, lady!"

"It's long overdue time to take down that group," said Jen, laying down her book and crossing the room to look over Frankie's shoulder. "Have there been any recent posts?"

Frankie scrolled down through the thread. "No, nothing since the cottages were sold. I did get that private message from Rose, remember?"

Jen's face stilled. "Yes, you showed me it. I think it was her saying goodbye, wasn't it? Just after she was released from prison, and moving to live with her daughter till she could find her own place?"

"She said she was leaving the group, changing her email and mobile phone numbers, and didn't want any contact from Irene," Frankie replied. "I messaged her back at the time assuring her we wouldn't pass on any of her details to Irene, and wishing her well. I hope she's doing ok and moving on with her life."

"It was all so sad," said Jen, taking Frankie's hand. "I didn't like Sam, and she caused mayhem, but still, to die like that..." she tailed off, her thoughts drawn back to Sam's funeral, the court case, then the subdued goodbyes with the women she'd come to know and like, and the ending of a dream.

Frankie put her arms around the woman she loved. "Of course it was dreadful, it was horrible! Sam dying, Rose in prison, her and Irene's lives wrecked too, us all uprooting, but Jen, we wouldn't have met otherwise, you wouldn't have found Johnny! Not to mention Jo and Maureen getting together, who would have guessed that would happen?"

Jen smiled faintly. "It wasn't all bad, of course not. I felt sorry for Elaine in all of that, losing Archie when she's finally found some happiness."

Frankie cut in: "Elaine is one of life's survivors, Jen. She and Archie had good times, a loving relationship and peace. It was so cruel that he was taken from her like that, just when they were settling into their new life, of course it was, but she emailed me recently to say she's made some friends and is enjoying life in Manchester, especially being near to her grandchildren. She's teaching hairdressing part time at an FE college and got involved with the local Women's Aid group."

"That's Elaine for you," smiled Jen. "One of life's grafters! Talking of grafters, we should have Johnny and Ross over for dinner soon. They seem to be spending every spare moment doing up the house and maybe they could do with a night off and some proper food!"

"It's hard to cook with no kitchen," Frankie chuckled. How many more weeks till that's done? Three, is it?"

"Yep, and then they'll be starting on Ross's photography shed, or whatever they plan to call it!"

"I'm astonished how well Johnny's taken to a domestic life," said Frankie, smiling. "He was always neat and tidy, and organised – I used to drive him crazy with my messiness – but he's settled down so well with Ross, his racketeering days are certainly a thing of the past! It was really high time we both grew up, wasn't it?"

Jennifer said nothing for a moment, concentrating on stroking Misty, who'd climbed onto her lap and was purring vigorously. "You know when you're well off, don't you, old lady?"

Frankie looked at her. "Less of the old! Oh, you mean Misty!" She chuckled. "Right, let me get on with closing this group. Should we put up a final message for everyone, do you think?"

Jennifer pondered for a moment. "No, just close it down. Sometimes you need to just simply end things, draw a double line, put in a full stop, and not prolong the agony any longer."

"If you're talking in code about Marion," said Frankie quietly, "that ended a long time ago, before I even met you. I got a real shock that day in John Lewis, remember, it was just before Johnny's wedding? Seeing her again, with her children, realising she was pregnant, which meant she'd been sleeping with her husband, all that was quite difficult for me.

"As you know, sexual jealousy is ultimately the hardest hitting of all jealousies, that's the one that grips your guts, thinking of your lover with someone else, doing with them what you did with them… let me finish, please Jen, you don't need to say anything…although that incident threw me, took me back to that time with her, it's something which happened and is over, many years ago. Without a doubt, although I once loved her deeply and passionately, it is a long time ago, it's in the past. I can't go back and change it, and maybe I wouldn't want to, even if I could."

Jennifer said nothing, and Frankie continued, quietly: "I believe that our lives are a tapestry, which we add to each year we live. It has coloured panels where events or people or experiences were great, good, sensational, sad, disturbing or traumatic. The section on my life's tapestry which I experienced with Marion is a gold panel, but it's also shot through with scarlet threads, which stand for my bleeding heart." She paused, leaned over and took Jennifer's hand. "Your panel on my life's tapestry is solid gold, my darling."

They kissed, with no more words spoken, then Frankie turned back to her laptop, and worked silently for a few minutes. She closed the lid, purposefully, and took off her glasses, putting them with a snap into their case.

Looking across at Jennifer, the woman she loved, and planned to stay with as long as they both should live, Frankie smiled. "That's it done," she said. "The chapter's closed."

***

In Angus, the winds blew hard and strong down through the Glens, just as they'd done for centuries, battering through the small towns, villages and hamlets, rushing through gardens and along streets, blowing off hats and lifting washing line sheets into fresh scented sails, and bearing with them ominous flurries of the first snows and the threat of another winter gathering its strength. The thick grey clouds closed over the faint slits of blue in the sky, a looming menace in their gathering power. At Barleyknowe, the cottages sat silently, waiting…

The End

Printed in Great Britain
by Amazon